SEA STAR

ORPHAN OF CHINCOTEAGUE

'*Sea Star* continues the story of the wild ponies of Chincoteague. Misty is still there with Paul and Maureen and the wonderful old Grandma and Grandpa Beebe. The author can describe the magnificent characters of these simple people in few words. All children of 8 up will be enthralled by this book whether they are horse story addicts or not.

Wesley Dennis has illustrated the book with soft, rhythmic pictures that seem to move to the beat of hooves. An outstanding book, *Sea Star* is indeed a worthy successor to the earlier story *Misty of Chincoteague*.'   *Junior Bookshelf*

In *Sea Star* 'all the charm of stories about horses is here, with picturesque details of life at a pony ranch; the animal round up; Misty's new career as a film star; and the struggle to save the new young colt.'   *Coventry Evening Telegraph*

First published in 1949 by Rand McNally & Co
First published in Great Britain by William Collins Sons & Co Ltd
First published in Armada Lions 1972 by William Collins Sons & Co Ltd
14 St James's Place, London SW1

Third Impression August 1974

Printed in Great Britain by
Richard Clay (The Chaucer Press) Ltd, Bungay, Suffolk

TO IRVING JACOBY

CONTENTS

Last Pony Penning, I went to Chincoteague a second time. My purpose was to work with the movie men who were planning to film the book of *Misty*. I had no thought of writing another Chincoteague story. *Misty*, I thought, was complete in itself. Let the boys and girls dream their own wonderful sequels.

And then all my resolves burst in mid-air. Early on the morning after Pony Penning, a lone colt with a crooked star on his forehead was found at Tom's Cove. His mamma 'lay on her broadside, dead.'

Except for the sea mews and the striker birds, the colt was quite alone, one little wild thing, helpless against the wild sea.

And there, in that wild moment at Tom's Cove, the story of Sea Star was born of itself.

M.H.

1. BRAIDS AND RIBBONS

Paul was separating each silver hair in Misty's tail. At his feet lay a little pile of blackberry brambles which he had removed, one by one.

With an air of secrecy he looked around quickly to make sure no outsider could overhear what he was about to say. But he and his sister, Maureen, were quite alone in the barnyard of Pony Ranch – except for the wild fowl and the ponies. There was no need at all to whisper, but Paul did whisper, and he seemed to be laughing at a private little joke of his own.

'How'd you like to see Misty's tail braided?'

'Braided!' Maureen dropped the gunny sack with which she was brushing Misty's coat and stared. 'How silly! Whoever heard of a wild Chincoteague pony with a braided tail!'

'Nobody except you and me.' Paul looked around again, chuckling to himself. 'Nobody'll ever know except the guinea hens and ducks and geese, and who listens to them?'

Surprise crept into Maureen's voice. 'How'd you guess, Paul?'

'Guess what?'

'That I've been hankering to do Misty up like those pictures we saw in the paper, the ones of the horses at the big show?'

Paul laid the comb he had been using on Misty's rump.

'Mental telegraphy, of course. Miss Vic says when two people think the same thing it's mental telegraphy.'

'She does?'

'Yes. And I believe it!' Paul's voice no longer whispered. It chortled in amusement. 'For two nights now I've been dreaming Misty was a famous steeplechaser, and we had to braid her tail and mane and trim off her fetlocks and whiskers and clean her coat until if you patted her hip you couldn't raise a single puff of dust. Not a puff.'

Maureen dipped a corner of the gunny sack in a pail of water and began scrubbing Misty's knees.

Her words came jerking out to the motion of the scrubbing. 'We'll tie her braids with fancy ribbons. We'll put a wreath of flowers round her neck – like Grandpa says they do at the big races over on the main.'

Paul giggled. 'Grandpa'd say we're chuckleheads, but let's do it, anyway! Then we'll take pictures in our mind, and afore anyone else sees her we'll shake out her tail and her mane and let the wind rumple 'em all up so she looks exactly like a Chincoteague pony again.'

Though scores of ponies came and went on Grandpa Beebe's Pony Ranch, Misty stayed. For she belonged to Paul and Maureen. They talked to her as if she were human, and often it seemed that she talked back! Now, as if she understood their plans, she spun around, kicked the comb from her back, burst through the unfastened rope fence, and headed for the marshland, her mane tossing in the sea breeze.

Disturbed by her motion, the barnyard went wild with noise. Guinea hens, geese, ducks – wild ones and tame ones flew into the air with a great clatter. A bunch of ponies in the corral who, a moment before, had been dozing in the sun, alerted and were off, following the silver direction-flag of Misty's tail.

'My stars!' laughed Maureen. 'That Misty's got the sharpest ears and the knowingest mind of any pony I ever did see. Look at her. She's gone wild as her mother – bucking and leaping and kicking her heels at our plan.'

Watching Misty, Paul and Maureen thought a moment of her mother, the famous wild Phantom on near-by Assateague Island. Then Paul said, 'But Misty is not really wild; in two minutes she'll be back, asking for those braids and ribbons.'

10

Maureen did quick little capers of her own, mimicking Misty. She stumbled over the pail, spilling out half of the water before she rescued it. 'Look at her!' she said, a little out of breath. 'She's the same colour as the flowers of the kinks bush. And she floats on the wind, like they do.' A note of anxiety showed in her voice as she went on. 'You think the other ponies get jealous of Misty?'

''Course not. They don't ever get jealous of a leader. Grandpa says it's the first time he's seen a mare colt to be the leader.'

They watched the older ponies trying to follow Misty's antics. The more Misty galloped and bucked and twisted her body into the air, the more Paul's and Maureen's laughter rippled out over the marshland of Chincoteague Island.

'The big ones are clumsy as woods cows beside our Misty!' Maureen said.

Now Paul threw his head back and let out a shrill whistle. It was as if he had roped Misty with his voice. She jammed to a halt. Her head and tail went up. Then she wheeled and came flying in, the rest of the band stringing out behind her.

Maureen and Paul ran for the gate. When the entire bunch was safely inside, they fastened it securely.

Misty flew on past them to the entrance of her stall. There she settled down to earth like a bird after flight. She watched the other ponies go to a big open shed which they shared. Then she stood waiting at her manger, waiting for the little reward of corn and the pleasant scratchy feeling of the gunny sack.

Maureen went back to work, this time on Misty's muddy hocks. 'We got to hurry, Paul,' she said, 'before Grandpa gets back from Watson Town. I promised him I'd do Grandma's work today.'

Paul did not answer Maureen. His words were for Misty's furry ears. 'You're fierce and wild and wonderful when you come in all blown, your nose snortin' white flames like a dragon. I wonder if even Man o' War could have been as exciting looking.'

Maureen stopped scrubbing and stood up in thought. 'No, Paul,' she said slowly. 'I reckon even Man o' War didn't have as much fire.'

Misty, impatient with all the talk, moved over to a wash tub that was turned upside down and placed her forefeet on it. 'Here, you!' she seemed to say. 'Do I have to do *all* my tricks for a few kernels of corn?'

She lifted a forefoot high, pawing the air.

Paul caught it and shook it vigorously. 'How do, Misty,' he said, bowing very gravely. 'I failed to see you in church last Sunday. Hope you weren't ailing.'

Misty lipped Paul's straw-like hair to see if there was any taste to it. Finding none, she nudged his head out of the way and reached for the niblets of corn that he now produced from his pocket.

From all over the farmyard chickens and hens came running, pecking up the little kernels Misty dropped.

'Now she's clean and had a good run; so we can ready her for the show,' Paul said. 'That is, if you can find any ribbons.'

Maureen was in and out of the weathered house beyond the corral before Paul had three strands of forelock ready to braid.

'Here's lots of ribbons,' she called. 'They came tied around Grandma's presents when she was in the hospital. She

brought them home for me to do my hair, but I've been saving them up for Misty.' She spread them out on the upturned wash tub. 'Let's use all different colours.'

Misty liked the attention she was getting. She preferred the company of humans to that of the other ponies. They tried to sneak her ear corn, and nose into her water barrel.

But the boy and the girl – they neither snatched her food nor drank her water. They brought it instead!

She nipped their clothes playfully as the friendly, awkward hands braided and looped her mane and forelock.

'My fingers get all twisted,' Paul complained, 'but if stable boys over on the main can do it, so can I.'

'Why, your braids look better than mine, Paul. You've looped yours underneath instead of over on top. But my bows are tied better, I think. Now let's do her tail.'

Misty snatched little colt naps as they worked on her tail. A fresh wind from the sea fanned her face. It fluttered the ribbons on her forelock and mane. Every little while she would shake her head and make the braids dance. Then she would give a high horse-laugh into the pleasant July morning.

When the tail was tied in red and pink and blue ribbons, Maureen went off to gather an armful of flowers from the patch of Bouncing Bess at the side of the house. The stems were thick and strong, and she braided them so that the flower heads came close together, making a huge pink wreath.

'It's funny,' she thought to herself, 'I've done this often in my mind. The Bouncing Bess. Grandma's ribbons. The skinny little braids. It's as if we'd planned it all out together.'

On the way back, she tried the wreath around her own neck.

'Prettier than a wreath of roses, don't you think, Paul?'

'Bigger, anyway,' he said.

Together they placed the flowers around Misty's neck. Then they stood back, running their eyes over the picture before them – the wreath hanging down almost to Misty's knees, the tiny silver braids with dozens of gaily coloured bows.

Paul grinned broadly, both a little ashamed and a little proud of his handiwork. 'Jumpin' grasshoppers! No one

14

would know her from a blue ribbon winner. Why, her pedigree is bursting out all over!' He half-closed his eyes, reciting, 'Misty – out of the Phantom by the Pied Piper.'

'Who before that?'

'Pied Piper out of the Wild Wind by the Wild Waves . . . Out of . . .'

Maureen's laughter bubbled. 'We haven't got time to go all the way back to the ponies that swam ashore from the wrecked galleon. Come on! Let's make believe I'm the man who leads the winner before the grandstand, and you're the jockey.'

A handful of ribbon lay at Paul's feet. Quickly he picked out a wide band of purple satin and fastened it across his shirt like a jockey. Then he climbed up close to Misty's withers so he would not be too heavy for her. He bowed to the imaginary crowds, bowed again and again, as Maureen led Misty around the corral. Now he was accepting the imaginary silver cup while the people went mad with applause. He closed his eyes, listening to the sound of it. It was deafening. It roared and roared in his ears until they hurt.

'Paul! Paul!' Maureen shouted above the noise. 'Open your eyes. It's a plane. Heading towards us. It's going to land. Paul! Right here at Pony Ranch!'

2. THE SILVER PLANE

Paul started from his daydreams. Misty was trembling under him, prancing in fear. He slid off and blindfolded her with his hands. The spear of light in the sky was a silver plane. It came darting in, landing down meadow, taxiing towards them.

As it settled to a stop, three men scrambled out. One stayed with the plane. The other two came walking toward Pony Ranch, looking around and about them like men who had suddenly landed from Mars.

Maureen gazed awe-struck. 'Reckon something's the matter with their engine?' she asked.

Paul looked and gave a nod. 'Or maybe they meant to land at the Government base on the other side of the island.' He turned Misty loose and started for the plane at a dead run. Maureen was close at his heels.

Now that the whirring monster was still, Misty was full of curiosity, too. Ears pricked forward, she jog-trotted along-side Paul and Maureen, the wreath bobbing against her chest. The other ponies followed at a cautious distance, but when they reached the gate, Misty drove them back. Then she rejoined the boy and girl.

'It's like history,' Paul said as he ran. 'Columbus and his party lands and the natives go out to meet them.'

Maureen laughed nervously, 'They don't look to me like faraway people.'

Now the two men and the boy and girl were close enough to study each other. Uncertainly they all stopped in their tracks and stood very still on the narrow spit of land. In the sudden quiet the sound of rustling grasses and channel waves skipping into shore grew loud and distinct.

Paul and Maureen waited, listening.

'Good morning,' said one of the men, with a smile as warming as sunlight.

'How do,' nodded Paul and Maureen solemnly.

The man who had spoken was low-voiced, and his blue eyes were very young and very old. The look he gave them was not the look a grownup gives to boys and girls, but one that friends save for each other. 'My name is Van Meter,' he said, 'and this is my associate, Mr Jacobs.'

Mr Jacobs was a tall man, and his eyes were dark and deep like the sheltering coolness of a pine grove. 'How do,' he said, repeating Paul's and Maureen's way of greeting.

Misty broke the awkward pause that followed. A bug flew into her nose and she snorted it out so fiercely that her braided forelock flew straight up.

They all laughed and the strangeness was gone.

'This must be Pony Ranch,' said Mr Jacobs, looking at the fences and sheds as if he carried a blueprint of them in his mind.

'It is!' exclaimed Maureen.

'And you must be Paul and Maureen Beebe.'

The boy and girl nodded in wide-eyed amazement.

'But this pony,' said Mr Van Meter, his eyes taking in the wreath of Bouncing Bess and the braids and ribbons, 'it can't be! No, it can't possibly be – Misty!'

Paul picked up a piece of marsh grass and twiddled it between his fingers. 'It *is* Misty,' he said, embarrassed by the silly ribbons and wreath.

Mr Van Meter was plainly disappointed. As he turned his head he caught a glimpse of a little herd of wild ponies frisking along the beach of neighbouring Assateague Island. He gestured toward the wind-blown creatures. 'I expected to find Misty with her mane and tail blowing in the wind,' he said, talking more to himself than to the others. 'And I hoped she'd have some of the mystery of the sea in her look.'

'Oh, but she does!' exclaimed Paul and Maureen together. Quickly they lifted the wreath of flowers from her neck and began loosening her braids.

Maureen glanced up shyly as she worked, 'We just wanted to see how she'd look if she won a big race over on the main.'

'And how *do* you think she looks?' asked Mr Jacobs.

The boy and girl were shaking out the strands of hair.
'You say, Maureen.'

'No, you, Paul. Do you like Misty all prissied up with ribbons and things?'

Paul answered easily. 'Even before we started, we knew we'd like her better with her mane and tail free.'

'Good! So do I.' Mr Van Meter smiled with his eyes. 'Now, will you take us to meet your Grandpa Beebe?'

'He's gone up the island to Watson Town. Grandma's been having trouble with her biddies, and he wanted to talk to Miss Vic about them.'

'Oh.'

'He sometimes gets hung up talking,' explained Maureen, 'but nearly always he comes back pretty quick.'

'Perhaps,' suggested Mr Jacobs, 'we could talk to Mrs Beebe until he gets back.'

Paul shook his head. 'She's gone to Richmond with Clarence Lee.'

'Yes,' added Maureen proudly. 'Our uncle, Clarence Lee, Jr., is going to go to college. He may learn so much he could be a preacher!'

The strangers seemed to be turning matters over in their minds. There was a little pause before they spoke. 'Perhaps you would like to hear our mission,' Mr Van Meter finally said.

'Oh!' Maureen looked surprised. 'Are you missionaries?'

Paul snorted. ''Course not, Maureen. Whenever are you going to grow up? Mr Van Meter means that maybe we'd like to know why they came to our island. And how they know all about us and Misty,' he added.

Maureen blushed. 'Please to come and sit down on the benches underneath the pine trees,' she invited politely.

Together they walked over to the pine grove at the side of the house while Misty, free of her wreath and halter, kicked up her heels and trotted off to sniff and snort at the strange silver bird resting on her private exercise ground.

The two men watched her with a pleased expression. Then Mr Van Meter took a snapshot out of his billfold and passed it to Paul and Maureen. 'These are my two children,' he said. 'Last Christmas they were given a book that told the legend of a Spanish galleon wrecked long ago in a storm and how her cargo of Moor ponies swam ashore to Assateague Island, and how descendants of those ponies are living wild and free on the island today.'

Paul and Maureen looked up from the picture. 'That's just how it happened,' said Maureen.

'Don't talk, Maureen. Listen. Listen to what's coming. Maybe it's going to be something good.'

'It *is* good,' Mr Van Meter went on. 'My boy and girl kept telling me about the roundup of the wild ponies you people of Chincoteague have every year.'

'It's this week!' Paul blurted out.

Mr Van Meter nodded as if he knew all about it. 'Finally I got as excited as my children, so excited that I talked it all over with Mr Jacobs. We want to make a movie of it.'

Paul and Maureen just stared. They could scarcely believe their ears. A movie made about the wild ponies of Assateague! Then Maureen became thoughtful. 'Would Misty be in it?' she asked. 'She was born on Assateague,

21

but she's not wild any more.'

'That's why we are here, We'd like to use the real Misty in the picture, the little colt that was in the book.'

Now Maureen clapped her hands for joy and Paul leaped to his feet, letting out his shrill whistle. Misty came flying in, asking questions with her ears. He whispered the good news to her, laughing to see her ears swivel this way and that, as if to catch every word he was saying. Then she was off again, circling the plane and browsing all around it as if she were afraid it might eat her grass.

'We knew you'd like it,' said Mr Van Meter. 'That's what we came to see your Grandpa about. We want to buy Misty.'

'Buy her!' Two heads jerked up as if they were on puppet strings.

'Yes, we'd like to take her back to New York in that plane – on Friday after Pony Penning. You see,' he explained, 'the roundup scenes over on Assateague and the swim of the ponies across the channel we want to make down here. But all the close-up scenes could be done better in our studio in New York. It will take months, because colts can't work long at a stretch.'

'But why,' Paul cried, 'why would you have to *buy* her?'

'Because,' Mr Van Meter said soberly, 'we'd want to keep her a while after the screen play is made. We'd want to take her to schools and libraries where boys and girls could meet her. We'd want to fix a stall for her in the theatres where her picture was showing so that they could see the real Misty. It might be a long time before she could come back.'

'Yes,' added Mr Jacobs, 'and you are grown up enough to know that we would have to buy her to carry out our plans. We would have to be responsible for her.'

The two men were like jugglers. But instead of balls, they were using words, tossing them back and forth over Maureen's and Paul's heads. Always the words seemed out of reach.

Mr Van Meter said, 'We had a feeling you might want to share Misty with boys and girls everywhere.'

'Boys and girls who have never seen a real pony,' Mr Jacobs continued.

It was Mr Van Meter's turn now. 'Sometimes when I hear children in New York talk about Misty, it seems she no longer belongs to a boy and a girl on an island, but to boys and girls everywhere.'

The words kept flying, back and forth, higher and higher. 'Misty has grown bigger than you know,' Mr Jacobs said. 'She isn't just a pony. She's a heroine in a book!'

Paul pounded his fists against the rough hard bark of a pine tree. Maureen turned her back on the men, digging her bare toes in a bed of moss.

'There, now,' comforted Mr Van Meter, 'if you do not want to sell her, we will think no less of you.'

A silence came over them all. It grew deeper and deeper. Even the hens and the chickens stopped scratching, and far down the marshland Misty lay down to sleep.

The sound of a chugging truck was welcome relief.

'That'll be Grandpa,' Paul said.

Grandpa Beebe brought the truck to a stop. He got out and squinted down meadow at the silver plane. He took off his battered hat and scratched his head in puzzlement.

'Grandpa! Oh, Grandpa! Come!' Paul and Maureen shouted, panic in their voices.

Grandpa came swinging towards them. 'What you two bellerin' about?' he yelled right back at them. 'Ye sound like a couple bull calves caught in a bob-wire fence.'

'Oh, Grandpa,' cried Maureen, throwing herself on him, 'they want to make a movie of Misty, and they want to buy her and take her away. Oh, Grandpa!' The words lost themselves in great heaving sobs.

Grandpa put Maureen away from him. He strode over to the two men and faced them eye to eye. 'If I was a younger fella,' he exploded, shaking a gnarled forefinger at them,

23

'I'd give ye more'n a battle of words. Ye should be down-right ashamed o' yerselves. Grown men come to hoss trade with childern! Oncet when I was a mere little boy in my nine I went out to Hog Island and I come upon some nestes, fish hawks' nestes they was, and I stole some eggs outen 'em. That night I woke up in the dark and I felt mean and shrivelled inside. And that's how you two should feel now.'

The men started to speak, but Grandpa waved for silence.

'Why, Paul and Maureen here has raised Misty from a teensy baby. I reckon Misty figgers they're her pappy and mammy.' He clapped his hat on his head and looked from one to the other. 'Why, Paul here saved Misty from drownding and oncet he stayed a hull night in a truck with her, and him and his sister bought her with their own

earned money. You city fellas maybe wouldn't understand, but livin' out here on this lonely marshland, why,
Misty's the nighest to a friend these childern got.'

'But, Mr Beebe, we do understand –' Mr Jacobs started
to say more, but Grandpa turned his back and talked to the
boy and girl.

'Mind the time Misty got in the chicken swill and et all
them green apple peels and got the colic? Mind how we
three had to stay up walkin' her and walkin' her all the
night long?'

Maureen blew her nose.

'I do, Grandpa,' Paul said. 'And I recomember last
Christmas when we fixed cardboard antlers to Misty's ears
and slung two gunny sacks with toys pokin' out of 'em over
her back. Recomember?'

'I do!' Maureen spoke up. 'And she had holly berries tucked in her mane and jingle bells tinklin' from her halter.'

Grandpa Beebe's voice gentled like a thunderstorm turned into a spring rain. He included the two strangers in the circle now. 'Yep,' he chuckled. 'We took her right smack into the church for the children's Christmas party. You should of heard the childern laugh to see a pony in church. But one o' 'em spoke up mighty cute. No bigger than a turnip that kid weren't, and his voice was jest a mouse-squeak, but he come up to Misty an' he said, ''The little Lord Jesus was borned in a stable, and He'd like as not let a pony come to His house.'' Then Misty passed the presents around from her packs.'

'Stop!' cried Mr Van Meter. 'Can't you see the more you tell us about Misty the more we want her?'

But Paul and Maureen and Grandpa went on as if they had not heard. 'Mind the time we brought her into the kitchen,' Paul asked Maureen, 'and Grandpa was washing his face over by the mirror, and when he looked up there

was Misty laughing over his shoulder?'

Grandpa slapped his thigh. 'I tell ye, fellas, 'twas the funniest sight I ever see. I looks up at that shaggy face in the mirror and thinks I to myself, "Great guns, I'm gettin' whiskery!" '

Grandpa cut his laughter short. 'What in tunket am I laughin' at? This ain't funny! Now you two strangers tell yer story and be right smart quick about it. Me and Paul got to go down the peninsula today.'

Mr Van Meter looked to Mr Jacobs and Mr Jacobs sent the look back. 'You tell it, Van. You have children of your own.'

Patiently, Mr Van Meter told the whole story from start to finish. He explained, too, that his company was young and struggling and could afford to pay only two hundred and fifty dollars for Misty. 'But,' he added quickly, 'if the children do not wish to sell her, we shall think no less of them.'

'Thar's yer answer, then. We'll help ye all we kin with yer picture-making, but Misty's next to the Bible with us. Why, she's got the map of the United States on her withers, just like her wild mommy, the Phantom.'

'And,' added Mr Jacobs very quietly, 'the marking on her side is in the shape of a plough, like the state of Virginia.'

Grandpa looked surprised. 'Call her in, Paul.'

Paul let out his shrill summons. It roused Misty from her sleep. She listened for the whistle again. This time it came louder. She thrust her forefeet in front of her, got up sleepily and came lazing in.

Grandpa took hold of her forelock. He turned her around.

'By smoke!' he exclaimed. 'She *has* got the marking of Virginia on her. The shape of a plough it is.' He grew tongue-tied for a moment. Then he smiled. 'I'm sorry I was snappish and made such a big to-do. But,' he added sternly, 'the answer is still no.'

27

'Grandpa,' suggested Paul, 'don't you figure they could find a good colt to buy at the Pony Penning sale after the round-up?'

' 'Course you could,' Grandpa told the men. 'And Paul and Maureen'll help ye all ye want during Pony Penning time. They'll be glad to run yer errands and tell ye where the ponies will be druv, and where they'll be swum acrost the channel. Now we got lots of work to do. Maureen's got to do the cookin' for her Grandma, and me and Paul have got big business down to Cape Charles.' He started to walk off. 'You two goin' up in that air buggy or could we drop ye off uptown?'

'We'd like a ride to the inn uptown,' Mr Van Meter told Grandpa. 'Our pilot friend is anxious to be off for Norfolk as soon as he finds out if we are welcome here.'

'Well, ye're welcome to go about yer picture taking, all right. Come along. We'll go down and tell yer friend. Then I'll drop ye off at the inn.'

3. A MILL DAY

Maureen went into the house. It was hard to settle down to her chores until the plane was gone. She heard its engines warming, heard it roar down the point of land. She ran to the window to see it take off, blowing the grass into ripples behind it.

Two cameras and a little cluster of luggage were left behind. Paul and Grandpa, Mr Van Meter and Mr Jacobs, each picked up a load and carried it to the truck. Now the truck was moving away too, and soon Pony Ranch was bathed in silence.

Maureen put on Grandma Beebe's apron, wrapping it twice around her and tying it in front. The breakfast dishes were still on the table, beds unmade, rugs rumpled on the floor. She looked around, wrinkling her sunburnt nose. 'I'd rather clean out the pony stable and all the chicken coops than clean house!' she thought to herself.

But it was seldom Grandma Beebe left Pony Ranch, and Maureen had promised to take her place. She lighted the flame under a big pot of beans. Then she stood in the middle of the floor thinking.

'I wonder –' she said out loud in the quiet of the house. 'No!' she stamped her foot. 'No, we couldn't sell Misty. We just couldn't.' And she turned briskly to the unmade beds.

Meanwhile, Paul and Grandpa had left the two men at the little frame inn and were driving across the causeway, leaving Chincoteague Island far behind.

All the way down the long peninsula to Cape Charles no mention was made of Mr Van Meter and Mr Jacobs. It was almost as if they had never dropped out of the sky at all.

'Mighty nice cabbages in that patch,' Grandpa would say. 'And the 'taters'll soon be ready to dig, I reckon.'

'Uh-hmm,' Paul would answer. 'How many ponies you figure to sell down to Cape Charles, Grandpa?'

'Oh, a whole flock, likely. Tim Button wants to use 'em to hawk his garden truck through the streets.'

'Grandpa?'

'What is it, boy?'

'Why do the people over on the main say *herds* of ponies, and we say *flocks*?'

'Why!' thundered Grandpa, taking one hand off the wheel to rub the spiky white whiskers in his ears, 'it's 'cause Chincoteague ponies is different, that's why. They fly on the wind like birds. But,' snorted Grandpa, 'the horses over on the main – they be earthbound critters.'

Pleased with the answer, the boy fell silent.

A truck cut in ahead of them. It was packed solidly with dark red tomatoes. Paul counted the crates, guessing at the number of tomatoes in each, then at the total tomatoes in the truck.

The day was slowly ravelling itself out. Big Tim Button had changed his mind about wanting to buy the ponies. 'Sorry, Beebe,' he twanged through his nose, 'but I just signed some papers to buy a couple secondhand trucks.' And he threw out his chest, slapping the papers in his pocket as if he were not sorry at all.

Tired and discouraged, Grandpa and Paul headed for home. On the way they stopped at the ferry station to pick up Grandma and her friend, Mrs Tilley, just back from Richmond. Paul had to climb into the body of the truck to make room for them.

He made believe he was a pony being shipped away. He could poke his nose right into the cab because a colt had already done that and broken the glass in the window. Paul looked between the beards of wheat that decorated Grandma's hat and giggled to himself. If he were a pony now, he would rip off the wheat and eat it. Then, like as not, he would trample the hat.

He looked at Grandma to see if she would mind. But her eyes were absently following the fields along the road. He doubted if she would care at all. Mrs Tilley, however, was lively as a wren, chattering and wagging her head, opening her purse, shutting it again, fussing with her packages. She would fly into a fit if a pony ate her hat. Paul grinned at the thought.

Then he turned his back and sat down quickly to squelch the idea. He dangled his feet over the tailgate and watched the road unroll like a bolt of white ribbon behind them.

It was almost sundown when they turned in at Pony Ranch.

Grandma sniffed audibly as soon as the truck door

opened. 'Paul! Run into the house, quick. The pot of beans is burning!'

Heavily, she got out and walked up the steps into the house. Maureen met her. 'You got the best smellers in the whole world, Grandma! The beans were just fixing to burn, but you saved 'em.'

With a kiss and a pat, Grandma whisked off Maureen's apron and tied it around herself. 'There!' she sighed, 'I'd sooner have bread and molasses and burned beans to home than fine vittles on the main.'

At supper that night when Grandpa had finished his plate of beans and spooned up every drop of molasses, he turned to Grandma. 'How about yer trip, Ida? How does it feel to have a boy in college?'

'I – don't – know,' answered Grandma, with a long pause after each word, 'I just don't know.'

'Well, where's Clarence Lee, Jr.? Ain't he got hisself all enrolled in that fine school?'

Grandma exchanged a glance with Grandpa, then nodded her head toward Paul and Maureen as if she did not want to discuss the matter in front of them.

'Oh,' chuckled Grandpa, 'if it's the childern ye're worried about, ye can forget them. They done a heap of growin' up today.'

Grandma put down her fork. 'I would feel better maybe if I did talk things out,' she said, looking from one to the other. 'They were mighty nice to me there at the school.' She paused, then rushed on. 'But the tuition money – it's got to be paid ahead of time. Seems like the school is so overcrowded. There's more young men want to enrol than there's places for 'em to sit down.'

'Why can't they bring in stools and folding chairs,' interrupted Grandpa, 'like we do when the church is full?'

'I spoke of that, but they just smiled at me.' Grandma let out a big sigh. 'I've had a mill day, Clarence. Seems like my heart's been tromped on. I did so want Clarence Lee to go to college and be a preacher.'

'Where's the boy at now?'

'He stayed to Richmond, trying to raise the money. But, Clarence, I'm all worried up. He's got to take some kind of tests and he's trying to earn a pile of money at the same time. Some boys can work hard and study too. But they ain't had the bad pneumonia. Besides, most of them just get the gist of what they're studying. Clarence Lee, now – well, he's got to go deep down.'

'Ye say a pile of money, Ida. How much do ye mean, exactly?'

'Three hundred dollars.'

'Three hundred dollars!' echoed Grandpa.

'I know, Clarence. The grass was late coming this spring, and ten of your best mares died off. I know. . . . But it was a pitiable sight to see him walk out that door, looking lost and lonely, like a colt cut out from a big bunch of his friends.'

'Dang it all!' raged Grandpa. 'Ef only Tim Button had taken them ponies. All I got to my name is fifty dollars.'

Paul and Maureen had long since stopped eating. They looked up from their plates at the same time and suddenly their glances locked. Then, white-faced, they nodded to each other.

'Grandma,' Paul spoke very quickly, as if he were afraid he might change his mind, 'two movie men were here to-day. They came to buy Misty.'

'For two hundred and fifty dollars,' added Maureen.

Grandma's coffee cup was half way to her lips. She set it back down again without touching it.

'You didn't sell her!' she exclaimed, aghast.

'Well, practically,' Paul said. 'As soon as they give us the money.'

'You see, Grandma,' Maureen explained very carefully as if she were talking to a little girl, 'Misty really doesn't belong just to us any more. She's grown bigger than our island. She's in a book, Grandma. Now she belongs to boys and girls everywhere.'

'Yes,' Paul's voice warmed. 'They want to take her to schools and libraries for children to meet – children who've never seen a real pony.'

'I should think you'd have wanted to horsewhip the men,' Grandma said to Grandpa.

'Oh, he did, Grandma, but when they told how much Misty meant to poor little city children, well, what could he do?' asked Maureen.

Paul sat up very straight, thinking out his words carefully. 'We want to give the money to Uncle Clarence Lee,' he said, 'and when he gets to be a great big preacher, maybe he'll want to send Maureen and me away to school.'

'And if he does,' came Maureen's high voice, 'I'll study to be a horse doctor.'

Grandpa seemed to have a choking spell. He pulled out his red bandana handkerchief; it almost matched his face.

'Consarn it all,' he spluttered and gulped, 'I must of got one of them kinks-bush catkins in my gullet.'

'Clarence, did you *let* the children sell Misty?'

Grandpa Beebe took a long time folding his handkerchief and getting it back into his pocket. Then he looked sideways, from Paul to Maureen and back again. He cleared his throat. At last he said, 'What else could I do, Ida? Misty is theirn. Besides, them men was dead right!'

The silence around the little table seemed never-ending. It was Grandma Beebe who broke it, speaking very softly. 'Now I know what you meant, Clarence, when you said the children done a heap of growing up. They had a mill day, too.'

Again the silence held them together while each one braved his own thoughts. Suddenly, a sharp siren pierced the quiet. It went through the house like a streak of lightning.

Grandma clutched the table in alarm.

'Don't be so twitchy, Ida. You know that was just the fire

whistle calling volunteers to ready up the Pony Penning Grounds.'

'Oh, I plumb forgot about all the big doin's.'

'Grandma,' asked Maureen, 'could I go with Paul to help the firemen?'

Grandma laughed, but there was a catch in her voice. 'Tonight I guess I'd let you move the sands of the White Hill if you had a mind to. Go along. All of you. I got a mighty big letter to write to Richmond.'

4. THE PICTURE-TAKERS' PLANS

Out the kitchen door, down the steps, through the barn-yard, Paul and Maureen ran.

Geese and turkeys, guinea hens and chicks, flew out of their way. Pigs ran snorting and squealing into the pens. But the ponies came running toward them, jostling each other to be first. Some pinned their ears back, driving the others away. To them Paul and Maureen meant good things. Corn. Water. A good hard gallop.

Misty bustled in among the other ponies, scaring them away with her threatening teeth. She wanted to get closest to Paul and Maureen.

'You're the littlest one,' Paul whispered, 'but you act the biggest.' He laced his fingers into her mane and led her into her own stall. For a second his face tightened. 'Maybe,' he told her, 'when you come back from New York, you'll be old enough for me to ride.'

He dropped a handful of corn into her feed box and while she was busy nibbling it, he quickly closed the door behind her.

Maureen had already bridled Watch Eyes, the pony with the white eyes. She held another bridle out for Paul.

'We got to find Mr Van Meter and Mr Jacobs before they meet Grandma,' she said.

Paul took the bridle. He sorted the ponies with his eyes and selected Trinket, a lively mare, taller than the others. He slipped the reins over her head and the bit into her mouth. He fastened the cheek strap. Then he vaulted up, ready to go.

Grandpa, pitchfork in hand, came to see them off.

'Ye done a big thing,' he said, his eyes warm with admiration. 'We can't keep nobody to the end-time, anyhow. They got to grow up. And usually they got to go away.' He shoved his pitchfork in the soil and cleaned off the tines slowly to help his thinking. 'Now the way for us all to take the sting off our thoughts is to keep busy as hummer-birds. We got to get so plumb tired we can't lay awake by night. We'll jes' turn in, turn over, turn out. That's what I'm going to do!'

Fastening the gate, he brandished his pitchfork over his head and was off, singing in a husky voice,

> *'Oh, they're wild and woolly and full of fleas,*
> *And never been curried below the knees. . . .'*

Down the lane, along the hard-packed trail to the Pony Penning Grounds, Paul and Maureen rode. The sun was slipping into the pocket of the horizon. Dusk was gathering, but Watch Eyes and Trinket knew their way. Often they had been entered in the races during Pony Penning Week. When they reached the grounds, they turned in of their own accord.

'You're early for the races,' a man in a fisherman's cap laughed up at Paul and Maureen. 'By the way, did two men find you? I understand they're picture-takers, come all the way from New York.'

'They here now?' asked Paul.

The fisherman pointed his finger toward the pony pens. 'They're down yonder in the big pen, conferencing with the fire chief.'

Paul and Maureen could see them now. Mr Jacobs sitting on the fence, writing in a notebook, Mr Van Meter nodding to the fire chief while his eyes wandered over the empty pens and out across the water to the masts of the oyster boats.

Paul and Maureen rode up to them. The faces of the men turned quickly.

'Hello, you two,' Mr Van Meter called.

The fire chief mopped the sweat beaded on his forehead. 'I'm mighty relieved you've come,' he said. 'Wilbur Wimbrow just asked me for a wiry somebody to do a special job for him. That's you, Paul. And the ladies of the Auxiliary need you to help wash dishes in the dining hall, Maureen.'

'We did come to help, Chief,' Paul answered, fixing his eyes on the ground, 'but mostly we came to tell the movie men we changed our minds – about Misty.'

Mr Jacobs hastily stuffed his papers into his pocket and looked up with a startled expression.

Mr Van Meter ran a fingernail across the rail of the fence to scratch out his thoughts.

'You – you haven't changed your minds?' asked Maureen in sudden alarm.

'I don't know,' said Mr Van Meter. 'Your grandpa, how does he feel about it?'

'Why,' gulped Paul, 'he told Grandma at supper tonight that you were dead right.'

Both children nodded, not daring to trust their voices.

Mr Van Meter put out his hand. He reached up and took Maureen's first, then Paul's. 'It's a deal, then,' he said in a very quiet voice, 'and I think you know we'll take the best possible care of Misty. We'll fly her to New York the day after Pony Penning.'

Paul and Maureen counted the days in their minds. They had less than a week.

After a little while Paul said to the fire chief, 'We'll tie Watch Eyes and Trinket. Then we want to go to work.'

The fire chief saw the look in their eyes. 'Wilbur Wimbrow is over near the track, Paul,' he said with understanding. 'He's having trouble installing the loud-speaker. And the ladies are cleaning the cupboards, Maureen. Seems like you two must have sensed how shorthanded we were tonight.'

All that week, day after day, Paul and Maureen spent at the Pony Penning Grounds, helping Chincoteague get ready for its big celebration. Paul liked working alongside the volunteer firemen. They were broad-shouldered and strong; yet they treated him as if he were one of them. When they needed someone to squeeze into a small spot, they never said, 'We could use a youngster here.' Always it was, 'Paul, he can do it for you. He's wiry as any billy goat.'

Once or twice Paul caught himself whistling as he worked. Then suddenly in the midst of a tune he would remember, and fall silent.

Maureen worked in the hall where the huge Pony Penning dinner was to be served. All the dishes had to be washed, and fresh white paper tacked on the long tables. Cutting and tacking the paper was fun, but washing the stacks upon stacks of dishes unused since last Pony Penning seemed a waste of time to her. 'Why don't we just dust them off?' she suggested in a small voice.

When everyone laughed, she slipped away to Pony

Ranch to help Grandpa. She found Mr Jacobs there, sitting in the doorway of the corn house, taking notes on the backs of old envelopes.

'Could I ask something?' she said shyly.

Mr Jacobs looked up and gave a friendly nod. 'I'd like that. Ask all the questions you want.'

It was always hardest to begin. Maureen twisted one leg about the other uncomfortably. 'Is New York,' she blurted out at last, 'is New York a place where the sea winds blow?'

Mr Jacobs answered quietly and earnestly. 'Yes,' he said, 'but not as softly as here.'

'And could a pony – I mean, could a body smell the sea?'

Mr Jacobs' eyes grew deep and thoughtful. 'Yes, sometimes. But you've got to sift it through city smells. It's far away, like something in a dream.'

Misty butted right into their conversation. Grandma's white curtains were on the line, and Misty had swooped under them. Now she came waltzing along, trailing the curtains far out behind her like a wedding veil.

This sent Maureen and Mr Jacobs off into peals of laughter, and brought Grandma out on a run. She caught up her curtains to wash them all over again without so much as a cross word for Misty.

The days flew by, but the night-times did not go quickly at all.

'Did you hear a lot of owls whooing last night?' Maureen asked Paul on the morning before the roundup.

' 'Course I did. Anyone would hear screechy critters like that. But what was even louder was the apples making a thud when they fell.'

'Do you . . . do you hear them, too, Paul?'

Paul nodded. 'I counted eight. And twigs a-snapping like rifle shots, and the ponies tearing the grass as noisy as Grandma ripping old bed sheets to make dust rags out of them.'

In the midst of their talk, Mr Van Meter came driving up

40

in an old rented car. He got out and sat down on the kitchen stoop so that he was looking up at them.

'We plan to take the roundup scene tomorrow,' he said. 'We're anxious to get good shots of the roundup men driving the wild ponies to Tom's Cove over on Assateague Island. You've been on the roundup, Paul. You'll know where we should set our cameras. Will you help?'

Paul lifted his chin and stood up very straight. 'I'll help,' he said.

'Mr Jacobs will go with you,' Mr Van Meter went on. 'But I'll be waiting here on Chincoteague to get pictures of the ponies swimming across the channel. Maureen, will you help me? You could tell me just where the ponies will land.'

'I have to be here,' Maureen answered. 'After the wild ponies are swimmed across, I always help drive them into the pony pens.'

'Good! Then everything's settled. Paul will meet Mr Jacobs at Old Dominion Point at seven-thirty sharp, and I will meet you there a little later, Maureen.'

The boy and girl nodded politely.

'It'll be just as exciting as going on the roundup,' Paul said, but his words were braver than his voice.

'It's funny,' Maureen confided to Paul after Mr Van Meter had driven away, 'instead of hating Mr Van Meter and Mr Jacobs, I like them. I like them both.'

'I do, too,' admitted Paul. 'And sometimes when I hear Grandma brag on "Clarence Lee at college" I feel good inside.'

'Like the time you turned the wild Phantom loose and let her go back to Assateague?'

'Yes, like that,' Paul said.

5. CAUGHT IN THE PONY-WAY

On the dawn of the roundup day, Paul tiptoed to his window. He crouched on the floor, his arms resting on the sill. A full yellow moon, flat as a tiddlywink, hung low in the western sky. A greyness was rising in the east and the sea, too, was a ball of grey cotton. It was the hour the roundup men would be leaving Chincoteague, loading their mounts onto the scow that would ferry them over to the island of the wild things.

In his mind Paul could hear the sound of the motor and the waves slapping against the heavy timbers of the scow. He could hear the blowing and snorting of the horses, the clipped, nervous speech of the men. Once he had been one of them. Single-handed, he had captured the wild Phantom and her baby, Misty. How long ago that seemed! He wondered if the Phantom would be caught this year. His body broke out in a sweat just thinking about her. How beautiful she was! How hard he and Maureen had worked to tame the wildness out of her! But in the end they had given her back her freedom.

'Some critters is made to be wild,' a voice said behind him.

Paul scrambled to his feet, startled.

It was Grandpa Beebe in his nightshirt. 'I couldn't sleep for thinkin' about Misty's mamma,' he said. 'So I tipped to yer room. Figured ye might be awake.'

'Grandpa!'

'Yes, boy.'

Paul's words came in a rush. 'Grandpa! If you hopped Watch Eyes and galloped to the mooring place, you could stop the scow. You could join the roundup. You could,'

Paul whispered tensely, 'you could make sure the Phantom escaped.'

The little bedroom was very still. Paul could not see Grandpa's face, but he could hear his troubled sigh.

' 'Tain't like ye, Paul,' Grandpa said at last. ' 'Twould be downright dishonest. Besides, when the roundup men comes upon the Phantom, they'll be puny as dustin' straws in a blow. Ye can almost count on her escapin' this year. She's been caught oncet. She ain't goin' to let it happen again. Now slip on your pants,' he said. 'Ye can help me do the chores afore ye have to meet the movie men.'

Sharp at seven-thirty Paul was waiting at Old Dominion Point. A few early visitors from the mainland were tramping about expectantly, asking questions of each other.

'How did the wild ponies get to Assateague in the first place?'

'When was the first Pony Penning held?'

'I heard it's the oldest roundup in the United States and the biggest wild west show of the east!' said a man with a Kodak in his hands and three children at his heels. 'It's different, too. They swim the wild ponies across to Chincoteague.'

Paul walked away. He could not bring himself to talk about the roundup and Pony Penning. 'It's sacred, kind of,' he said to himself. 'And it takes somebody like Grandpa or Miss Vic to make folks understand about it.' He was glad when he heard the chugging of a motor and caught sight of Joe Selby's oyster boat with Mr Jacobs and a stranger aboard. He rolled his pants above his knees and waded out into the water.

'Halloo-oo-oo,' he shouted, waving his arms. 'I'm here!'

The boat nosed over and he clambered aboard. Mr Jacobs was barefoot, too, and he was ripping open cartons of films.

'Paul,' he said, 'this is Mr Winter, one of our cameramen,

who came down to Chincoteague last night.'

Paul looked up at the lean, serious young man. His shy 'how do' was lost in the sputter of the engine as the boat turned and headed out into the channel.

'And you know Joe here,' Mr Jacobs nodded toward the man at the tiller.

Paul smiled at the weather-creased face of Joe Selby. Many a time he had gone oystering in this very boat.

'I hear Grandpa Beebe is a pretty good weather prophet. What did he say, Paul? Clear skies?' asked Mr Jacobs, squinting anxiously at the clouds.

Paul blushed. 'I didn't ask him.' How could he explain that he and Grandpa had been more concerned with Misty's mother?

'Well, Joe here thinks it won't rain. Never has rained on Pony Penning Day. Never will, he says.'

The talk stopped.

The wind dried Paul's wet legs. He shivered a little from cold and excitement. He watched the people on Chincoteague blur into a cloud, then watched the cloud slowly wisp out until it stretched far up the beach.

Ahead of him lay the waving grasses of Assateague, and on and beyond the pine woods and the sea. If he half-closed his eyes, the tops of the pines became the mane of a horse and the White Hill the cap of a rider, and the whole island was riding in advance of their boat, looking after her like any out-rider, protecting her from the mighty waves of the Atlantic.

Suddenly the motor went quiet, cutting off his thoughts.

'We're in the shallows now,' Joe called out. 'Close as we can get to Tom's Cove.'

Camera on shoulders, film held high above the water, the two movie men jumped overboard.

Paul followed. The soft bottom squinched up between his toes. How different this was from going on the roundup! Instead of pounding over the marshland, shouting and

45

driving the wild ponies, here he was, splashing ashore, as peaceful as on a Sunday school picnic.

But Mr Jacobs was not calm and quiet, and his eyes were no longer dark and cool. They threw sparks like horseshoes on a pavement.

'Paul,' he said sharply, 'from which direction will the ponies come? We want to set our cameras close enough to catch the wild look in their eyes.'

Paul thought carefully before replying. 'The roundup men drive 'em down to that little grazing ground yonder. But they come from' – he wheeled around and pointed a finger to the deep woods that formed the backbone of the island – 'they come from . . .'

Paul's sentence hung in mid-air. A rolling boom of noise! Dust clouds swirling! And hulking out of the woods some dark misshapen thing! It might have been a prehistoric monster or a giant kicking up clods of earth for all the form it had. But whatever it was, it hugged along the ground like puffs of smoke on a windless day. Now the shape fell

apart! It was the men on horseback driving the wild herds to Tom's Cove. They were coming earlier than anyone had expected. Much earlier.

Paul and the two men were blocking the pony-way! The ponies would be coming right at them. How could he get the men and the camera to safety?

A daring thought crossed his mind. Let them stay in the pony-way! Let them stay! Let the wild things come dead-heat at the camera. 'They got horse sense,' he thought. 'They'll split around us.'

He skinned off his white shirt and buried it in the sand. The ponies must not shy away from a billowing white object.

'Follow me!' he shouted, running directly toward the noisy, swirling mass.

The cameraman was young. He could run almost as fast as Paul, even with a clumsy camera to carry. Along the hard-packed sand, across the meadow marsh, up a little rise the three of them ran.

'Here!' shouted Paul, pointing to the camera.

It was too late to explain his plan. The dark racing monster was no longer a nebulous thing. Wild ponies and men on mounts were taking shape, coming around the horseshoe curve of Tom's Cove, splitting the air with yells and whinnies and pounding hooves, like thunder rolling nearer and nearer.

Mr Jacobs was standing close to the cameraman, his eyes darting nervously from the oncoming ponies to the overcast sky. He nodded to Paul that he understood. If the plan worked, the ponies would break up in two bunches around the camera. He would get a close-up of the wildest scene of the roundup.

And suddenly the sun struck through the clouds like a powerful searchlight. Manes, tails, sweating bodies were high-lighted with red and gold.

'Now! Now!' Paul heard himself yelling. 'This is it!' Why was that cameraman so slow? What was he waiting for? Was there ever a sight so wild? It was wilder than thunder and lightning. Wilder than wind.

He clenched his hands behind him to keep from knocking the camera over. This man Winter was as cold as his name. Paul hated him. He had given up going on the roundup for him, for a man who stood frozen. A man who waited, waited, waited, when all around him the wild things were blowing and screaming.

And just when he could stand the delay no longer came the clicking, clicking sound of the camera close in his ear. Mr Winter was grinding now. And just in time. The ponies were plunging at him, their eyes white ringed, their nostrils dilated until the red lining showed like blood. Now they were splitting in two bunches, swerving around the camera, coming so close that their tails whisked it.

Paul drew a long breath of relief as he turned to look at Mr Jacobs.

'He knows just when,' laughed Mr Jacobs weakly.

6. HORSE-DOCTOR PAUL

The ponies began to slacken their pace. They were coming to the sweetest grass on Assateague. The roundup men, almost as blown as the horses, drew rein.

Suddenly Paul forgot the cameramen; he was a horseman now. 'Look!' A choked cry escaped him. 'A mare's hurt, terrible hurt. Look at her limp. Her colt can outrun her.'

He raced across the wiry grass to the men resting their mounts. 'What's the matter of her, Mr Wimbrow?' he called anxiously.

Mr Wimbrow took off his fisherman's cap and wiped the perspiration from his forehead. 'Heel string's cut,' he said tiredly. 'Likely she cut it on an oyster shell.'

The mare tucked her forelegs beneath her and lay down to rest, as if she knew the roundup was only half over. She was a pinto with splashy black and white markings. She might have been beautiful, but now she was just a crippled captive. A captive who seemed content to rest while her puzzled colt and stallion watched over her.

'You going to swim her across the channel?' Paul asked.

'Reckon we will,' Mr Wimbrow said. 'The salt water will clean the cut better'n any man-made medicine.'

Paul nodded. If Wilbur Wimbrow thought swimming wouldn't hurt the mare, it wouldn't. He turned to study the milling mob of ponies, watching the stallions gather in their own families. Every now and then a mare would break away, and the stallion would herd her back into his band with galloping hooves and bared teeth. At last they were all neatly grouped like classes in school.

'I hanker to see the Phantom,' Paul thought aloud, 'but I hope I don't!' He wondered at himself. One time he had so

49

wanted to capture her. Now he so wanted her to remain free. He could not bring himself to ask the men if she had been caught. From one bunch of ponies to another he went. There were blacks and chestnuts and bays and pintos, but nowhere among them was Misty's beautiful wild mother with the white map on her withers.

'She didn't get caught!' he whispered with a fierce gladness. He wanted to throw back his head and whinny his relief to the whole wide world.

Instead, he belly-flopped in the grass, laughing softly to himself. The sun poured down on his back, warmed him through. All around, the wild creatures were grazing, their legs scissor blades, opening and closing, opening and closing, as they moved from one delicious clump of grass to another. Paul felt strangely comforted. Out here on Assateague, with the wild things so near, he could push aside unhappy thoughts. Maybe Friday would never come. He pulled a blade of grass and slid it between his teeth, savouring the salty taste. For a long time he lay quite still,

lulled by the wind and the waves and the pleasant sound of the ponies cropping the grasses. It was not until he heard boats starting up their motors that he went back to the cameramen.

'The tide's ebbing bare,' he told them. 'The men'll be driving the ponies into the water soon. They're going to need all the boats to make a kind of causeway for the ponies to swim from Assateague to Chincoteague.'

He dug up his shirt, shook it free of sand, and pulled it

over his head. Then he waded out to Joe Selby's boat.

Everything was working according to plan. The boats, spitting and sputtering, were lining up to form a sea lane across the channel. On the beach the roundup men were closing in, drawing a tight circle around the ponies. A sudden explosion of lusty yells, and now the animals were plunging into the sea! Men's cries mingled with the screaming of ponies and the wild clatter of birds overhead. The channel was boiling with noise.

Paul's eyes and ears sharpened. He felt he belonged neither to the roundup men nor to the cameramen. He was an excited onlooker, like the visitors from Norfolk, from Washington, from Philadelphia. He watched the hurt mare and her colt stumble into the foam. The water seemed to revive the mare.

'Look at her colt!' he laughed aloud. 'He's getting a free ride!'

Sure enough, the colt's muzzle was anchored firmly on his mother's back. It seemed to comfort the mare, to give her new strength.

Four or five tow-headed boys were swimming alongside the ponies. They wanted to be ready in case a foal needed lifesaving. They remembered how Paul had rescued the drowning baby Misty. But this year the colts were expert as swimmers in a water carnival, and not one needed help.

The first ponies were scrambling up the beach at Chincoteague now, their coats curried by the water and the noonday sun. The blacks were no longer shaggy and dusty but took on the shininess of satin, and the chestnuts glistened like burnished copper.

'Slick as moles!' Paul laughed to himself.

He wanted to get to them quickly, eager as any sightseer. 'Let's put in to shore,' he yelled to Joe Selby.

The scow with the roundup men was landing alongside them. Wilbur Wimbrow's arm went up, signalling for Paul to come.

The boy welcomed an excuse to be with the horsemen. 'They need me,' he said to Mr Jacobs as he leaped over the side of the boat.

'That hurt mare's got to have some first aid,' Mr Wimbrow told Paul. 'Your fingers are fine as a mother-woman's. Us men'll hold her quiet while you lay these cigarettes in her cut. The tobacco'll burn it clean.'

He handed two cigarettes to Paul and took the bandanna handkerchief from around his neck. 'You can use this for a bandage,' he said. 'It'll stay the blood.'

Grandpa Beebe, gathering his rope, stepped up behind Mr Wimbrow. 'Leave me rope the hurt mare fer ye,' he said.

Mr Wimbrow was glad of fresh hands to help. 'After we doctor her,' he told Grandpa, 'I'd like it if Paul and Maureen'd lead her over to my place. If she's driven to the pony pens along with the mob, she's liable to get tromped on.'

'Better off by herself,' Grandpa agreed. 'What you want done with her colt?'

'We'll drive him to the Pony Penning Grounds with the others. He's big enough to be sold with the other colts.'

Grandpa Beebe easily roped the mare. Then he talked to her in the voice he saved for wild things. 'Easy there. Easy, girl. Ye're not hurted bad.'

The crowds closed in to watch.

'Why don't they shoot her?' asked a well-meaning visitor wearing Oxford glasses.

'Why!' barked Grandpa. 'For the same reason yer family didn't aim a gun at ye when ye lost yer nacheral sight.'

The people cheered for Grandpa and pressed in closer.

'Go ahead,' Mr Wimbrow nodded to Paul. 'We got her.'

Paul tore the paper from the cigarettes. He picked up the hurt leg, bending it at the knee. Gently but firmly he laid the tobacco in the cut. It was good to be helping, not just watching. Now he knew how good Grandma must feel when she took care of a sick neighbour. Maybe he and Maureen would both be horse doctors when they grew up. Maybe they would live in the old lighthouse on Assateague. Then they could see whenever a wild creature was hurt. All these thoughts spun around in his mind as he tied the bandanna securely.

'Paul, you leg up on Trinket now,' Mr Wimbrow said. He beckoned to Maureen, who was mounted on Watch Eyes and holding Trinket for Paul. 'Then you two lead the mare down behind Old Dominion Lodge so's she can't see her colt go off without her.'

Grandpa and Mr Wimbrow tied a connecting rein between the hurt mare and Trinket and Watch Eyes. Then they faced her out to sea while the roundup men roped her colt and headed for the Pony Penning Grounds. A little moment and it was over. The trembling of the mare quieted. Her neighing became no more than a whimper. She limped numbly along between Watch Eyes and Trinket.

'Paul,' said Maureen as they headed for Mr Wimbrow's house, 'seems this mare's got enough trouble without having her colt taken away from her too.'

Paul was busy trying to hold Trinket to the slow pace of the mare.

''Course she's got enough trouble,' he said at last, 'but up to Mr Wimbrow's house she won't be able to hear the colt-whinkerin' for her all night long.' He rode on in silence for a moment. Then he added, 'Maybe it's like a twitch.'

'What's like a twitch?'

'Humpf,' snorted Paul. 'You wanting to be a horse doctor and don't even know what a twitch is.'

'I do too know what a twitch is. It's nothing but a piece of rope twisted around a horse's nose to make him forget where his pain's at.'

'Well,' said Paul, 'this mare's foot probably hurts so bad she can't fret about losing her colt.'

Maureen nodded her head.

7. THE BEST KIND OF WINKERS

Grandpa was already at home when Paul and Maureen arrived. He was trying to seem very happy.

'Childern,' he shouted, 'look-a-here. Ever see such a whopping big watermelon? And it's frosty cold, asides.' He held it high to show that it was beaded with icy sweat. 'Grandma says if we're going to eat it in our hands we got to stay outside.' He winked happily.

Grandma Beebe came out of the house with a pan of steaming water, a bar of brown soap, and washcloths. She set the pan on a bench in the shade. 'Now,' she said brightly, 'wash up good, and let the wind dry you off. I been making a plummy cake for the Ladies' Auxiliary and my kitchen's hot as a griddle. Out here it's nice and cool.' She looked up at Paul and Maureen. 'What's the matter of you two? You glued to Watch Eyes and Trinket?' But she smiled as she said it.

Paul and Maureen slid to their feet and led their mounts to the big shed.

'Don't let your ponies stomp on my biddies,' Grandma called after them.

There was a chorus of neighing as the horses that had been left behind greeted the ones that had been away. Misty's neigh was a high squeal of happiness. Paul and Maureen stopped to rough up her mane and stroke her nose. Then they hung up their bridles and joined Grandpa at the wash bench, while Misty tagged along.

'There's a letter come from Clarence Lee this morning,' Grandma was saying as she laid a red-checked cloth on the picnic table. 'He's in the college all right, studying to be a minister.'

A minister, eh?' Grandpa Beebe straightened up and planted his feet wide apart. 'I'm-a-danged,' he laughed softly. 'To think I sired a minister! Why, I'm that proud I'm liable to go around with my chest stickin' out like a pewter pigeon.'

'You mean pouter pigeon, Clarence.'

'Well, let's not gibble-gabble. We got us a lot of watermelon to eat. And I've brung some new little carrots for Misty.'

Grandma had made crab cakes and baked them in clam shells, and she had black-eyed peas and corn pone with wild honey. And Grandpa was all excited about the deep pink of his watermelon and the blackness of the seeds. ''Taint only something noble to look at,' he exclaimed, 'but whoever tasted a melon so downright juicy and sweet?'

Pony Ranch seemed to draw close about Paul and Maureen. They could not help feeling comforted by Grandpa's and Grandma's happiness.

Maybe, if no one thought about Friday, it would never come. Maybe they could go on picnicking forever, with Misty coming to them and offering to shake hands until all the carrots were gone, and the chickens fighting over the watermelon rinds and rushing for each seed that was dropped.

'I declare!' Grandma said, her eyes fixed on the whirling chickens. 'It took me to be a grownup afore I figgered out why they call that shoal up north of here "Hens and Chickens". It's plain as the nose on your face that they do it 'cause the water swirls and closes in like hens and chicks after a morsel to eat!'

Grandpa clucked his tongue in admiration. 'Ida! I never knowed the reason either!'

When the picnic was over. Paul got up and stretched himself. He squinted at the sky between the pines and found the position of the sun. 'They're just about fixing to call the bronc-busting contest over at the Pony Penning Grounds,' he said to Grandpa. 'Reckon I'll ride.'

Grandma caught her breath. 'Don't let him do it, Clarence,' she cried in alarm. 'He'll be killed outright.'

'There, there, Ida,' Grandpa's voice was the same one he had used on the hurt mare. 'He'll not get killed. Leastaways, not outright,' he grinned. 'Y'see, Ida, Paul and Maureen is like nervous hosses. They got to wear winkers to keep from seein' things comin' up from behind. My grandpap used to say' – and here Grandpa Beebe began rubbing the stubble in his ears as if he were enormously pleased with his memory – 'he used to say, "Clarence, keepin' busy is the best kind of winkers. If ye keep busy today, ye can't see tomorrow comin' up." That's what he said.'

Underneath his eyebrows Grandpa's eyes had a merry gleam. 'Go 'long, Paul. Pick out a tough pony and ride 'im till he's dauncy. I'd sure give my last two teeth to trade places with ye.'

8. A WILD ONE FOR
WILD-PONY PAUL

When Paul and Maureen rode into the Pony Penning Grounds, the loud-speaker was blasting at full strength. 'Ladies and gentlemen, Jack Winter of New York City is making his way over to the chute.'

'That's the cameraman!' Paul told Maureen excitedly. 'He's going to ride in the contest!'

They tied their mounts quickly, running to the corral just in time to see the young New Yorker come bolting out of the chute on a white spook of a horse. His hands were clutched in the horse's mane, and he was gripping hard with his knees. But his feet were not locked around the pony's barrel. He looked like a rider in the bareback class at a horse show.

Paul was screaming at him, 'Lock your feet around his belly. Lock your feet around . . .'

But his words thinned into nothing. The white spook had planted his forefeet in the earth and was lashing the sky with his heels. One second . . . two seconds . . . three seconds . . . four, five, six, barely seven seconds, and Mr Winter was plummeting through space, then falling to earth with a thud.

A bugle of triumph tore the stillness that followed. Then the freed animal went snaking around the corral until a round-up man roped him.

Shakily Mr Winter got to his feet, stumbled out the gate held open for him, and lost himself in the crowd.

'Give a big hand to Mr Winter, folks. That's all he'll get,' called the voice over the loud-speaker.

The crowd responded with spirited applause.

'Who'll be next folks? The ten dollars still stands. Who's next?'

Paul's arm shot into the air, but no one saw it.

The voice kept prodding. 'How about Delbert Daisy?'

People all around Paul and Maureen were making remarks. 'Delbert tried it last year,' someone said. 'He's too smart to try again.'

'I'm a cowboy from Texas,' a man with a ten gallon hat drawled, 'but I be dogged if I'm ready to pick me a homestead. I'm a reg'lar bronc rider, used to a halter and a belly rope for anchor.'

Another stranger agreed. 'No siree! No thousand pounds of wild horseflesh under me without something to hold on to. Not me!'

'Who's next, folks? Who's next?' the voice hammered.

The crowds around the corral were banked solid. Paul could not wedge between them to climb the fence. He and Maureen finally wriggled underneath it.

Inside the corral Paul's hand went up again.

This time everyone saw.

'Look, everybody! Paul Beebe's next,' the voice bawled out. 'Ten dollars to Paul if he can stay aboard for thirty seconds. Stand back, Maureen. That's his sister, folks. Stand flat against the fence, Maureen.'

Maureen clutched at her throat. They were going to let her stay in the corral! She stood back as far as she could, leaning hard against the rails, with the people pressing against her on the other side.

'Let out a wild one for Wild-Pony Paul!' came the voice.

Paul was gone. He was climbing the fence of the chute, swinging his leg over an unbroken pony, gripping the strands of tangled mane as if they were reins.

'Who's he riding?' someone cried.

There was a pause.

Then the announcer's voice cracked with excitement. 'A wild one it is! Red Demon – a she-devil on hooves. Those aren't her ears, folks, they're horns!'

A hush of expectation fell over the onlookers.

'Be you ready, Paul?'

A thin voice answered, 'Turn 'er loose.'

Every eye was riveted on the closed gate of the chute. Now it burst open and Red Demon, a chestnut with a blaze, shot out bucking and twisting. In a quick flash of seeing, her white-ringed eyes swept the corral. Suddenly she spied a tree at the far end. She hurtled toward it, not straight like a bullet, but in a tortuous, weaving line, calculating, deadly.

Paul tried to capture the rhythm of her muscles. He leaned back, gripping with his thighs, pushing inward and backward with his knees, turning and twisting with her, writhing like a corkscrew.

The crowd watched, horrified. This was the thrill they had come to see.

Maureen hid her face in her hands, listening. She heard the earthquake of hooves as the Red Demon headed for the tree, heard a man's voice rasp out, 'He's going to get hung up in that pine!' She waited for the crash, but there was none. Stealthily she peered between her fingers. They were not going to crack up! The wild pony was swerving around the tree and Paul was making the spine-wrenching turn with her. He was still on!

Now the weight of Paul enraged Red Demon. Birds and flies could be removed with a swish of the tail. But no mere swishing would remove this clinging creature. There had to be violence. She brought her head and shoulder to the ground, then jerked up with a sudden sharpness. The boy's head jounced down and shot up in unison.

A woman shrieked.

Maureen grabbed the back of her own neck. She felt as if it had been snapped in two.

'Hang on!' she screamed. 'Hang on!'

Red and glaring, the hot sun struck down on the two

wild things. It seemed to weld them together like bronze figures heated in the same furnace. They were all of one piece. The boy's arms were rigid bands of bronze, and his hair did not fly and toss with the rocketing of the pony – it hung down, sweat-matted between his eyes, like the forelock of a stallion. It was hard to tell which was wilder, boy or pony.

'Fourteen seconds . . . fifteen seconds,' the voice over the loud-speaker blared.

And still the two figures were one, the boy's arms unbending, his legs soldered in place.

That lone tree at the end of the corral! It seemed to bewitch Red Demon. Again she rushed at it, head lowered as if to gore it with her devil ears. A thousand throats gasped as she whiplashed around it again, and then once again, each time missing by a wink.

And still Paul held on.

'Twenty seconds . . . twenty-one seconds . . .''

The power of the sun seemed to strengthen as the seconds wore on. Now it fused the two wild creatures, making molten metal of them. In fluid motion, horse and boy were riding out the fire together. Together, they dipped and rose and spurted through space, now part of the earth, now part of the sky.

Maureen felt her knees giving way. 'Please! Please! Someone stop them! Oh, stop them!' She tried to brace herself against the fence to keep from falling. The beat of Red Demon's hooves continued to pound hard and steady in her ears. She closed her eyes for a second, then opened them.

Something was happening! The molten mass was bursting in two. Everything went black before her eyes. When next she opened them. Paul was lying beside her. Then they were both picking themselves up, laughing feebly. Paul was no longer the bronzed rider on a bronzed

horse. He was a dirt-streaked, pale-faced boy in faded jeans.

All about them half-frenzied visitors were swarming over the fence rails, men and women laughing and crying both, asking questions and answering themselves. And over and above the noise, the voice on the loud-speaker never stopped. 'Thirty-three seconds! Thirty-three seconds! Paul rode her dizzy. The ten dollars goes to Paul Beebe.'

9. OFF IN A SWIRL OF MIST

Paul spoke in breathless jerks as they edged away from the crowd. 'I'm going to give the ten dollars – to Mr Van Meter – to see that Misty has some carrots each day,' he told Maureen.

But Mr Van Meter refused the money. 'We'll see that Misty gets her carrots, Paul. You save your money for something very special,' he said with a wise look.

'What would that be?'

'I don't know, but something special always turns up when my youngsters have ten dollars saved. Now you two better go home. You've had a hard day.'

The sun was throwing long shadows by the time Paul and Maureen arrived back at Pony Ranch. There was not much talk during supper that night, and afterwards the boy and girl were too tired to enter Watch Eyes or Trinket in the night races to be held at the Pony Penning Grounds.

Paul helped Grandpa water the ponies while Maureen sat on a chicken coop drawing pictures of Misty. She worked with quick strokes because Misty seldom remained still. While the pony was drinking at the water barrel, Maureen drew a side view of her, the side with the map of the United States on it. And while she tagged after Paul, Maureen sketched a funny little back view – the softly rounded white rump and the long tail that swished from side to side when she walked. Maureen laughed aloud as she tried to put the swishes on paper.

Paul and Grandpa came to look over her shoulder.

'By smoke! I'm a jumpin' mullet if there ain't a strong favourance to Misty!' Grandpa said.

'It's not bad,' Paul agreed.

'Don't she look like a little girl wearing her grandma's long dress?' Maureen giggled. Then her face sobered.

Paul was staring at the pictures, at all of them. 'You can make me some – if you like,' he said in a low voice.

Misty went back to the water barrel for another long, cooling drink, then stood quite still watching Maureen sketch and erase and erase and sketch. The evening breeze was stirring. Soon Misty would settle down to the business of grazing by moonlight. But right now, when it was neither night nor day, she was content to snuff the winds and to look about her.

She came over to Maureen and breathed very softly down her neck. She nudged the bread board on which the drawing paper was tacked. Then, as if she were posing, she turned her head slightly, looking out over the marshland, waiting for night to close in.

Maureen sketched on. The pricked ears, the blaze on her face, the soft pink underlip with its few lady whiskers, the mane lifted by the small wind.

At last she had four pictures for Paul and four for herself. She started to say good-night to Misty, but Grandma was watching from the doorway.

'Let's see what you've done, Maureen,' she called out. 'As a girl I was always one for drawing, too.'

Maureen showed Grandma the pictures and smiled at her praise. Then she put the ones for Paul on a shelf in his room and went to her own room. There she laid her page of sketches on her pillow, and fell into a deep, exhausted slumber.

Toward morning, sounds pecked at her sleep. She dreamed she was riding Red Demon on an oyster-shell

road, and the tattoo of hooves pinged sharper and sharper in her ears.

She awoke to the sound of hammer strokes. With sudden anxiety she was out of bed, dressing, hurrying to join Paul and Grandpa. The hammer strokes could mean but one thing. They were building a crate for Misty. She must get to them quickly – to see they built it big enough, strong enough.

'If I don't have to eat any breakfast,' she pleaded with Grandma, 'I'll make up for it tomorrow. Honest I will.'

To Maureen's astonishment Grandma agreed. 'No griddle cakes this morning,' she said. 'They'd stick in your throat and lump in your stummick. Only this tiny glass of milk.'

Instead of an everyday glass tumbler, Grandma was pouring the milk in the ruby-coloured glass, the one her own grandmother had left her. Maureen somehow managed to drink all of it.

When she burst out of the house, the floor of the crate was already built.

'Maureen!' Grandpa called to her. 'You hurry down marsh and gather driftwood. Paul, you look in that bunch of scantlings. See if there's anything we can use. I'm a-danged if lumber around Pony Ranch ain't scarce as two-headed cats.'

The finished crate was an odd-looking object. Uprights had been splintered from an old gate, laths taken from a deserted chicken roost, and driftwood from who knows where; but so much care and measuring had gone into the making of it that to Paul and Maureen and Grandpa it did not look rough-made at all.

'Snug, ain't it?' said Grandpa, forcing a smile. 'And Paul's gathered a big enough bundle of salt grass to last her the hull day.'

''Member when we readied the stall for Phantom?' asked Maureen very softly. 'Readying a crate is not . . . is not . . .'

Grandpa snapped his fingers. 'Consarn it all!' he sputtered. 'I plumb forgot the pine shatters. Paul and Maureen, you gather some nice smelly pine shatters from off'n the floor of the woods. Nothin' makes a better cushion for pony feet as pine shatters. Besides, it smells to their liking. *Every*thin'll smell to her liking – salt grass, driftwood, pine shatters.'

Taking the wheelbarrow and an old broom, Paul and Maureen headed for the woods.

'Grandpa can think of more things for us to do!' Maureen scolded as she swept the pine needles in a heap.

'It's just his way of putting our winkers on, Maureen.'

Scarcely were the pine needles dumped onto the floor of the crate than Grandpa pointed to the sky.

'Be that winged critter a gull or a plane?'

The beat of engines was the answer. A silver plane came sweeping down on Pony Ranch, now circling it, now banking, now turning into the wind, landing, taxiing right up to the gate!

Barnyard creatures flew screeching into the air. The older ponies ran snorting for their shed. Only Misty stood her ground. She had seen this strange silver bird before. She had snuffed it carefully from its big nose to its twin tails. There was nothing at all to be afraid of.

Mr Van Meter and Mr Jacobs jumped out of the cockpit. They nodded a good-morning to Grandpa, then came right over to Paul and Maureen.

'It makes it easier,' Mr Jacobs hesitated, then tried again. 'It makes it easier,' he said, 'knowing you two *want* to share Misty with boys and girls everywhere. Van and I were saying this morning—if we didn't know we were going to make thousands of children happy, we certainly wouldn't make two sad.'

'Maureen!' commanded Paul, and there was something of Grandpa's tone in his voice. 'Here's some corn kernels. You stand by the crate and slip your hand between the boards.'

Maureen did as she was told.

'Now hold out the nibbles and call to her.'

Maureen's voice faltered, 'Come along – little Misty,' she sang brokenly, 'come – along.'

Misty hesitated only an instant. Then she stepped onto the friendly pine needles and walked into the crate.

It took Grandpa and Paul, Mr Van Meter and Mr Jacobs and the pilot, too, to load the crate onto the plane.

Maureen stood watching, looking and thinking and trying not to do either.

Suddenly she felt a pair of warm arms folded close about her. She turned and buried her face in Grandma's broad bosom. 'Oh, Grandma,' she sobbed, 'I feel just like a mother who has borned many children. But Misty is my favourite. And it hurts to have her grow up and leave us . . . without even looking back and whinkerin'. She's –' Maureen burst into tears, 'she's even eating her grass!'

'She don't understand, honey,' comforted Grandma. 'She's just a young 'un, all excited in her mind. Children and ponies both get all excited with travelling and their boxed lunches. They seldom cry when they go off. It's the ones left behind does the bellering. Now blow your nose good and don't let Paul see you cry.'

After the crate was safely stowed inside the plane, the men came back out and looked from one silent face to another.

'Now we will say good-bye to you all,' Mr Van Meter said quietly. 'We will do everything we can to keep Misty well and make her happy. She has a big job in life now. She's got to be a sea horse more than ever, leaving a little trail of happiness in her wake wherever she goes. She's got work to do!'

'Please,' asked Maureen, 'always each night whisper in Misty's ear that we'll be here a-waiting for her when she's ready to come home.'

'Think of it!' said Paul with a crooked smile. 'Misty's the first one of the family to see our islands from the air.' He turned to Mr Van Meter. 'Do you suppose you could point out the White Hill to her from the air so's she could see where the Spanish galleon was wrecked?'

'I think we could, Paul.'

'Then you could tell her how brave her great-great-great-great granddaddy and mammy were; how they swum ashore from the wrecked galleon in a raging storm.'

'We'll tell her that, Paul.'

'Gee willikers,' Grandpa's voice cracked, 'git agoin' afore we changes our minds and hauls Misty back out.'

Mr Van Meter nodded. He signalled to the pilot to start up the engines. Then he and Mr Jacobs stepped inside the plane.

'And be careful,' bellowed Grandpa above the noise of the engines, ''bout letting big chunky kids ride Misty too soon. Recomember she's a young 'un yet.'

The plane nosed the wind and roared along the narrow spit of land, the sound of its engines deepening as it climbed. It passed over a lone, wind-crippled pine tree, then up and up and out across the channel, away into the blue distance.

'She's over the White Hill!' shouted Paul into the wave of silence that broke over them.

They watched until the plane was swallowed in a white cloud of mist.

'Now ain't that just like a storybook?' Grandpa crowed, while he rubbed the bristles in his ear. 'When Paul fust seed her she was all tangled up in a skein of mist, and now she leaves in a sudden swirl of it. Don't it ease the pain of her goin'?'

There was no answer. None at all.

'Don't it?' he insisted, pulling his hat down low over his eye. 'That is, somewhat?'

10. ALL ALONE AT TOM'S COVE

For the space of a few brief moments, the little huddle of those left behind stood rooted. Whether they still heard or only imagined they heard the purring of the plane, no one knew.

Grandpa let out a sigh that seemed to come from his boots. 'Hmpf! You folks can stand here a-moonin',' he said at last, 'but as fer me, I got to hyper along to the Pony Pennin' Grounds. This be one of my big days. Some of the strangers from over on the main may want to buy a partic'lar pony with a partic'lar markin', and might be I'll have jes' the one fer 'em. Come along, Paul and Maureen.'

Paul shook his head. 'If you don't care, Grandpa, I don't believe I want to see any ponies today.'

Grandma cleared her throat. 'Clarence,' she said, 'I promised the Ladies' Auxiliary to bring some oysters to the Pony Penning Dinner this noon and to fry 'em myself. If you can spare the children, I'd like to have them take the little boat and gather some Tom's Cove oysters for me. I want to be sure they're good and plump and right fresh out of the sea.'

Listlessly Paul and Maureen followed Grandma to the house. They put on their high rubber boots. They took the flannel gloves and the baskets she offered.

As they walked to Old Dominion Point, they stared blindly at the familiar sights. The beach was deserted now except for the little white striker birds tippeting along the shore on their red feet. The milling crowds of yesterday were gone. They were at the Pony Penning Grounds.

In silence the boy and the girl climbed in a small boat with an outboard motor. Paul cast off the mooring line. He started the motor. It sputtered and stopped. He tried again. This time it chugged evenly.

They were sculling the waves now, heading across the inlet. Paul looked dead ahead. He saw a fish-hawk strike the surface of the water in front of the boat, then rise again with a fish so large he could hardly fly with it. He saw the lighthouse of Assateague, like some giant's dagger stuck in the island to keep it from floating out to sea. A circle of buzzards wheeled low over Tom's Cove, making a racket that could be heard above the beat of the motor. Idly Paul pointed to them.

Maureen nodded. She cupped her hands around her mouth. 'Likely something dead. A shark, maybe,' she called to him.

'Something's alive, too,' he called back. 'It's keeping the birds from swoopin' down.'

Now they were so close to Tom's Cove they could distinguish the shrill chirring of the hawks and the high whistle of the osprey. Paul's indifference was gone.

'The live thing's a baby colt!' he cried.

He shut off the motor and beached the boat. He made a sun visor out of his hand. And there, not a hundred yards away, standing quiet, was a spindle-legged foal. It had a crooked star on its forehead. And as it stood there with its legs all splayed out, it looked like a tiny wooden carving against a cardboard sea.

Maureen spoke Paul's thoughts. 'He's like the little wooden colts Mr Lester makes for Christmas.' Then she looked down at the quiet thing lying in the sand. Her voice fell to a whisper. 'It's not a shark that's dead.'

'No,' said Paul, 'it's his mamma.'

They started out of the boat, but when the foal heard the *plash-plash* made by their rubber boots, he gallumphed away, fast as his toothpick legs would carry him.

'Don't go after him, Maureen. He's afeared. Stand quiet. Might be he'll come to us.'

Paul's plan worked. When no one gave chase, the foal minced to a stop, then turned his wild brown eyes on them. The crooked star on his forehead seemed to widen the space between his eyes. It gave him an expression of startled wonder.

A quiet stillness lay over Tom's Cove. Even the circle of birds had stopped their screaming. Paul and Maureen made no move at all. They stood as still as the wooden stakes that marked the oyster beds.

Cautiously, as a child who has lighted a firecracker comes back to see if it will explode, so the foal came a step toward them. Then another out of wild curiousness, and another. When Paul and Maureen still did not move, he grew bold, dancing closer and closer, asking questions with his pricked ears and repeating them with his small question-mark of a tail.

Paul's laugh of wonderment broke the spell. 'Say! He's somethin'! A fiery little horse colt!'

At the sound of Paul's voice, the foal took fright and shied so sharply that all four of his feet were off the earth at once. Then he high-tailed it up the beach.

'He's sassy for one so little,' Maureen laughed. 'How long do you reckon he's been alone?'

'Not long. His mamma 'pears too old to stand the running yesterday. She's got an F branded on her hip – belongs to the fire company.'

'What'll we do, Paul?'

'Don't know. I'm a-thinkin'.'

'Let's take him back and bottle-feed him.'

''Course we'll take him back! But how do we rope him without a rope? How do we round him up without a horse? And even should we catch him, how do we hold him in the boat? He'll be lively as a jumpin' bean.'

Maureen was fumbling in her mind for an idea.

'We got to gentle him quick,' Paul said.

'Grandpa says nothing takes the wildness out of a

creature like sea water.'

'That's it, Maureen! That's it! We'll drive him into the channel. Then we'll swim out and tow him in.'

Their eyes fastened on the colt, Paul and Maureen worked off their boots. 'You stay on this side of him,' Paul whispered excitedly. 'I'll circle wide around on the other side. Then we'll close in and drive him into the sea.'

The foal's gaze followed Paul as the boy went around him in a wide arc. Now the three creatures were forming the three points of a triangle, the colt at the tip and Paul and Maureen back at equal distances on either side.

Paul stopped, took a deep breath. Then like any roundup man, he gave the signal. His wild screeching whoop tore jagged holes in the morning. Quicker than an echo came Maureen's cry. They both charged the foal, arms waving and voices shouting at the top of their lungs.

The wild creature stood frozen an instant. Then he became a whirling dervish, spinning around and around in

an ever-smalling circle. The roaring humans were coming at him from both sides, closer and closer. With a gallopy little gait he headed out into the water.

Splashing after him, yelling at him, Paul and Maureen drove him out beyond his depth.

'He can swim!' gasped Maureen. 'Look at him go!'

For a few brief seconds the baby colt headed out into the deep. Paul and Maureen watched his tiny pricked ears and the ripple he stirred, making a little V in the water. Suddenly the ears drooped.

'Oh, Paul! He's done in!'

With long strokes the boy and the girl were swimming toward the foal. He was no longer a wild thing, skittering away from them, no longer a brave little horse colt pointing his nose to the sky. He was a frightened baby, struggling to keep from being sucked under. He wanted to be rescued. Exhausted with thrashing and kicking, he let the human creatures swim near. The girl's hand touched him, held his

nose out of water. The boy took a firm hold of his forelock. It was thus that the three of them came swimming back to shore.

'Maureen!' Paul spoke jerkily to get his breath. 'I'll hold Lonesome. You get our boots.'

Still holding the tiny forelock, he shook the water out of his own ears. The foal shook his head too, fiercely, as if he could match anything Paul did. Paul laughed at him, and strangely enough the colt let out a funny little laugh too, until Tom's Cove was a jubilant echo of human and horse laughs.

Now Paul placed his arms under the foal's belly and lifted him into the boat.

Maureen stood dripping wet, watching. 'Don't call him Lonesome,' she said. 'That's too sad of a name. Let's call him Sea Star.'

Paul seemed to be talking to himself as he took Maureen's rubber boots and pillowed the colt's head on them. 'Why, that name's exactly right,' he said. He burst out laughing again. 'An hour ago we didn't want to look at a pony. Now this orphan has wound himself around us just the way sea stars wind themselves around oysters.'

'Oysters!' clucked Maureen. 'We plumb forgot them.'

'Grandma won't mind,' Paul said. 'Or will she?'

''Course not. She'll say a new-borned colt without any mamma is a heap more important. But the ladies of the Auxiliary will mind; they're counting on Grandma's oysters.'

Paul found an old gunny sack in the boat and began drying off the foal. 'Tell you what, Maureen. We'll take turns watching Sea Star. You can watch him first, while I fill my basket. Then it'll be my turn to watch. Besides, the tide's slacking. Soon the oyster rocks'll ebb bare. Oysters'll be thick as pebbles. In no time we can fill our baskets.'

The little colt's sides were heaving as he lay in the bottom of the boat. Maureen knelt beside him, two wet creatures side by side. 'You're all done in,' she whispered as she

81

combed his mane with her fingers. 'Why, your mane's nothing but ringlets. It's curly as your tail – even though it's drenched.' She laid her head alongside his. 'I can hear your breathing,' she said. 'It sounds like the organ at church before the music comes out. I kind of feel like I'm in church. The blue sky for a dome. White lamb clouds.' She leaned over and traced the star on his forehead. 'My, how you'll miss your mamma!'

As if he understood, the little fellow bleated. He scrambled to his feet. When the boat swayed, he tried to plant his legs far apart like a sailor's. Then his knees buckled and he was lying on Maureen's boots once more.

In the distance Maureen could see Paul scrambling over the rocks, picking up oysters, quickly throwing them into his basket. Now he was running back, his basket full.

'It's my turn to watch Sea Star,' he called out.

Maureen put on Paul's wet boots. They were too big, but she did not mind. She sloshed along in them, singing at the top of her voice.

> 'Periwinkle, periwinkle,
> Come blow your horn;
> I'll give you a gold ring
> For a barrel of corn.'

Paul sat on the edge of the boat, fondling the colt with his eyes. Occasionally he looked out toward Maureen gathering oysters. But he did not really see her. He was busy in his mind, thinking of the firemen's brand on the mare, thinking of the ten dollars he had won in the bronco-busting contest. He was buying the biggest nursing bottle they had in the store uptown. He was buying milk. He was giving Misty's stall to Sea Star. He was . . .

"Whee - ee - ee - ee - n - n - n!" Sea Star was drying out. He was hungry. He was crying his hunger to the whole wide world.

Maureen came running back. 'My basket's almost full,' she panted. 'Let's get a-going. Sea Star's got to eat.'

11. THE LITTLE TYKE

When Grandma Beebe looked out the kitchen window, she dropped the egg whisk in her hand and did not bother to pick it up, even though it was making little rivers of egg yolk on her clean swept floor.

She rushed out the door and stood on the stoop. Her mouth made an 'O' in her face as she watched the strange threesome turning in at the gate. Paul and Maureen looked to her as if they had been swimming with their clothes on. And wobbling along behind them on a lead rope made of vine was a tiny brown colt.

'We picked your oysters, Grandma,' called Paul.

'And we covered 'em all over with seaweed so they'd stay cool,' Maureen said, waving a piece of the seaweed.

Grandma did not seem interested in the oysters. She was looking right over their heads, clear over to Assateague, up to the place where the pine trees met the sky. 'The burden is all rolled away,' she said quite plainly.

Paul and Maureen caught each other's eye in surprise. They had half expected Grandma to look upon Sea Star as another burden. Instead, she seemed glad to see him! She was coming down the steps now, lightly as a girl.

'You been so long gone, children,' she said, 'I been beset by worriments. Now I know,' Her face broadened into a smile. 'You found a lone colt. Ain't he beautiful with that white star shining plumb in the centre of his forehead?'

'We had to drive him into the sea afore we could catch him,' Maureen told her.

'Land sakes!' laughed Grandma. 'You not only catched him, you gentled him! Here, hand me those baskets. I'll shuck my oysters while you make the little tyke comfortable.'

She took the baskets and disappeared into the house.

Paul carefully lifted Sea Star and carried him into Misty's stall.

'He's so tired,' Maureen said, 'he's not even whiffing around to get acquainted.'

It was so. Sea Star did not poke his nose into the manger nor smell the old dried cob of corn at his feet. He just stood, rocking unsteadily.

Paul was bursting with things to be done. 'I'll get fresh water, Maureen, and some of Grandpa's Arab feed mixture, and a bundle of marsh grass. You get milk from the ice chest, and see if Grandma's got a nursing bottle.'

Long legs ran excitedly in opposite directions.

'No,' Grandma pursed her lips thoughtfully in answer to Maureen's question. 'Yours was the last nursing bottle we had need for. I sent it away in the mission barrel.'

Maureen waved her arms in despair.

'But that's no never mind,' Grandma said quickly. 'I got a bottle of bluing here. We'll just rinse that out good, and we'll cut a finger off my white kid gloves for a nipple.'

'Oh, Grandma! Not your beautiful gloves Uncle Ralph sent you on Mother's Day?'

'The very ones. I don't wear gloves, anyway, only on a funeral or a wedding. It's lots more important that orphan colt gets some good warm milk inside him. He's all tuckered out.'

'He's spunky,' Maureen said. 'He ran away from us quick as scat.'

'You put some milk to heat and stir in a little molasses,' Grandma said. 'Between whiles I'll make as fine a nursing bottle as ever money would buy.'

A truck rattled into the lane and ground to a stop. Grandpa Beebe's booted feet came clumping up the steps and his voice carried ahead of him:

'Oh, they're wild and woolly and full of fleas
And never been curried below the knees . . .'

'Ida!' he bellowed through the screen door, 'the ladies is askin' when ye're comin'. Ain't ye ready?'

Suddenly he caught sight of the bottle. 'What in tunket ye two doin'? Don't tell me another grandchild's been left to our doorstep!'

'Why, that's exactly what happened,' laughed Maureen. She took Grandpa's hand and pulled him down the steps. 'Come quick, Grandpa! My sakes, you're harder to lead than a new-borned colt. Quick, Grandpa! Paul and me— we got the wonderfulest surprise for you.'

Grandpa let himself be pulled across the barnyard and into the corral and up to Misty's stall. Then he stopped dead. For a long time he just stood there staring from under his eyebrows as if he had never seen a newborn colt before.

A rapt smile slowly spread over his face. 'I'm a billy noodle!' he said softly. 'As purty a horse colt as I ever see.'

'Ain't he young?' asked Maureen.

Grandpa clapped his hands on his hips and grinned. 'That he is! Carries hisself in nice shape, too, for one so young.'

Paul explained. 'He belongs to the fire company. His mare was layin' on her broadside, right on the beach at Tom's Cove, Grandpa. Looked to be an old mare, white hairs growing around her eyes. We got ten dollars, Grandpa, and I – we, that is – you reckon the fire company will let the colt go?'

'Dunno, childern,' Grandpa answered. 'That's not what's important now. What's fust to my mind is, can anybody keep him? 'Tain't easy to raise up a baby colt without any mamma. Will he eat fer ye? Here, let me try that grass, Paul.'

Gently Grandpa placed a few wisps in the colt's mouth. He tried working Sea Star's muzzle. 'Go on, li'l shaver,' he coaxed. 'Start a-grindin' with yer baby teeth. First this-away, then thataway. 'Tain't half so dry when ye get to chawin' on it. And it's got a delicate salt flavour. Yer ancestors thought it was right smart good. Whyn't you jes' keep a-tryin'?'

The kitchen door squeaked open and Grandma's voice called out, 'Maur—een! Your milk's warm.'

'Coming, Grandma.'

Grandpa stopped Maureen with his hand. His clasp was so firm that the fingers left white bands when he took them away. 'Maureen, no!' he ordered. 'I oncet raised up a colt

on a bottle. 'Twas a horse colt, too, just like this one. And by-'n-by I couldn't poke my nose outen the door but what he'd come gallopin' at me, puttin' his hard little hooves on my shoulders, askin' fer his bottle.'

'I think that would be cute,' Maureen said.

'It *was* cute,' Grandpa admitted, 'that is, at first it was. I'd laugh at him and play with him, and like as not go back

87

in and warm up some milk fer him and put 'lasses in to make it taste mighty nice.

'But,' Grandpa's voice grew stern, 'when that colt was comin' on six month, 'twasn't cute any more. He got too sniptious for anything, and he growed so strong that when he put his hooves up to my chest 'twas like bein' flayed by a windmill. Why, if I didn't have something to give him he got ornery. Dreadful ornery. He'd nip and bite and have a reg'lar tantrum.' Grandpa sighed. 'Never could do a thing with that colt. Had to sell him up to Mount Airy to a dealer who wished he'd never clapped eyes on him.'

Maureen said wistfully, 'It would have been such fun to feed him, and poor Grandma's cut a finger off her new gloves and fixed up a nice bottle for him.'

'Well, you tell yer Grandma ter just sew that finger right back on! We ain't goin' to have no spoiled brat-of-a-colt around here. Our colts got to be nice and good.'

Paul bit his knuckle, trying to keep back the hot words. 'We're starving him, Grandpa. He'll die!'

'Shucks, Paul, we ain't even give him a chance. He'll be eatin' gusty-like afore sundown. Now here's what we'll do. I'll make a mash outa our Arab mix and leave it in the stall fer him, and he's got this nice salty grass, and a good bed to lie on, and the sea wind fluffin' up his mane.'

Grandpa picked up the bucket with the Arab feed mixture in it. 'Come,' he urged, 'you jest snuck away and let him be all by hisself fer a little while. Like as not he'll lay down and have a real refreshin' sleep, and when he wakes up he'll begin mouthin' things and find 'em good! He'll forget he's a baby and get all growed up in a hurry. I've seed it happen time and time again.'

'Does it *always* happen that way?' Maureen asked.

Grandpa grew tongue-tied. He stood, absently riffling the Arab mixture between his fingers. 'Most always, child,' he said at last. 'Now it's gettin' on fer dinnertime and I got to take yer Grandma to the Dining Hall. The ladies is a-waitin'.' He turned to go. Then came back. 'Hurry and change yer wet duds or folks'll think I grand-sired a couple mush-rats. Then ye can ride over to the dinner on Watch Eyes and Trinket. We'll leave the little shaver be. By the way, what's his name?'

'Sea Star,' said both children at once.

As they closed the stall door, Sea Star sent a high little whinny out after them.

'Ain't that cute?' chuckled Grandpa. 'He's a-whinnerin' fer ye already. My, but he'll be glad to see ye when ye come back. Ye're goin' to have a high-mettled horse colt there,' he added.

'That is, pervided the fire chief is agreeable to yer deal.'

12. RISKY DOIN'S

The smell of good things floated out of the Dining Hall –
oysters and clams frying, dumplings simmering in vege-
table juices, chickens and sweet potatoes roasting. The
steaming vapours ran like wisps of smoke past the noses of
the people waiting in line. The line moved slowly, like a
snake trying to wriggle into a hole too small for it. Paul and
Maureen and Grandpa were part of the line. As it crept
forward, Grandpa tried to make talk.

'Paul! Maureen! Stop yer worritin' and snuff up!' his
voice rolled out strong. 'Get a whiff of what I calls perfume.
Don't it make ye feel like a coon-hound hot on a scent?'

The boy and the girl did not need to answer. People all
around them were following Grandpa's advice – inhaling
the teasing odours in quick little sniffs, laughing and
agreeing with him.

Grandma's friend, Mrs Tilley, stood at the door taking
tickets. She greeted the Beebes warmly when they finally
reached the entrance. 'You three set up to this table right by
the door. It'll be cooler and you can see the visitors come in
hungry and go out full as punkins.'

The Dining Hall was a big, low-ceilinged building with
an endless number of long tables, covered with the white
paper Maureen had tacked on them. But now the white
was almost hidden by great serving dishes of golden
oyster fritters and clam fritters and crisp chicken and dump-
ling puffs and bowls of brown bubbling gravy.

Talk see-sawed back and forth from one table to another.
Home folks from the island and strangers from the mainland
were visiting like old friends. They all seemed to be
laughing, throwing their heads back, showing strong teeth

like colts, or teeth crowned with gold, or toothless gums, but all laughing.

Always, each Pony Penning time, it was the same. People on all sides of them laughing and making fun. But each year for Paul and Maureen there was a colt nagging at their thoughts, stealing their appetites.

A little white-haired man whose cheek pouch was bulging like a chipmunk's leaned across the table to Paul. 'I'll trouble you to pass me the chicken and dumplings, Bub.' He waggled his head toward the kitchen. 'If they're figuring eight pieces and four people to a hen like they useter do,' he piped in a thin voice, 'I'm goin' to discombobolate their figuring.'

Paul passed the chicken and dumplings.

Grandpa tried to lower his voice. 'Childern,' he smiled in understanding, 'jest 'cause somebody ter home is off his feed 'tain't no reason why ye should be off yers. Now let's us dig right in, and when we've slicked our plates clean so's Grandma and the other ladies kin tell we liked their cooking, then we'll hunt up the fire chief and ask him right out plain whether he don't think Sea Star was sent straightaway from heaven to take Misty's place.'

Maureen and Paul smiled back at Grandpa. He never seemed to fail them. They bent their heads over their plates and ate. To their surprise the food tasted good. The oysters were so slippery they did not stick in their throats at all. And they drank glass after glass of tea.

'I guess we had Grandma's fritters,' Paul said. 'Hers are the prettiest brown.'

After dinner the fire chief was nowhere to be found in the milling crowd, so Grandpa stepped up to the announcer's stand in the centre of the grounds. 'I'll thank ye to call out the fire chief's name in that squawker contraption,' he said to the announcer.

'Calling the fire chief!' the voice rang out above the noise of the people and the music of the merry-go-round. 'Calling

the fire chief! He's wanted at the announcer's stand.'

This brought the fire chief weaving his way through the crowd. He was nodding to visitors at right and left, and the cane which he carried when he was tired was nowhere in sight.

The people made way for him until he reached the stand. Then Grandpa Beebe stood in his path.

'Was it you wanted me?' the chief asked.

Grandpa nodded.

The chief's eyes crinkled. 'Clarence,' he said, 'ain't this the best crowd we ever had to Pony Penning? Weather's good, too, and everything's running along smooth as honey on a griddle cake.'

Paul and Maureen hung a little behind Grandpa. Paul

was tying knots in a piece of string, and Maureen stood twiddling her curls in the wrong direction. When the fire chief caught sight of them, he came a step closer and lowered his eyes to theirs.

'I know you two are feeling sad about Misty, but you done a fine thing. Besides, she'll come home swishing her tail behind her – maybe not for a few years – but one day for certain. Chincoteague ponies is like Chincoteague people. Once they gets sand in their shoes they always comes back.'

'That ain't what's eatin' 'em, Chief. I'll let 'em tell ye theirselves while I go make arrangements fer shipping one o' my ponies that's goin' all the way to Sandusky, Ohio.'

There was a little silence while the fire chief and Paul and Maureen followed Grandpa with their eyes. They watched him tack back and forth in the sea of people like a sailboat, his old battered hat the topgallant sail. When he was lost to view, Paul and Maureen suddenly felt adrift.

The fire chief drew them to a bench away from the crowd and motioned them to sit down, one on each side of him. Then he helped them with a question.

'You folks at the pony sale this morning?'

'No,' Paul answered. 'We were oystering over to Tom's Cove.'

'So?'

'Yes, sir.' Paul spoke quickly now. 'And lying on the beach was a mare with the brand of the Fire Department on her.'

'Was she solid brown, with no white on her at all?'

'Yes, sir.'

'Except she was getting white around the eyes,' Maureen spoke up.

'Was she a very good mare, Chief?' Paul asked.

'That she was! Raised up frisky colts. A new one each year. Always hers brought the highest prices at the auction.' The fire chief's voice had a faraway tone. 'Guess she helped buy a lot of equipment for the fire company,' he said. 'This year she and the Phantom were the only mares who didn't get rounded up. We figured the Phantom was too smart, but we feared for the brown mare.'

A slow tear showed at the corner of Maureen's eye. It grew fuller and rounder and finally spilled over.

'Come, come, child. That mare was full of years. She'd had the free and wild life for nigh onto fifteen years. Don't cry about her, honey.'

'I'm not. It's her new-borned baby I'm thinking about.'

The fire chief was silent for what seemed a long time. 'Hmmm,' he said at last. 'Had a colt, did she?'

'A baby horse colt,' Paul answered. 'A beauty! All brown except for a white star in the middle of his forehead. His name's Sea Star.'

A smile played about the fire chief's lips and his head

nodded as if he saw the spindly-legged foal standing all alone at Tom's Cove with the sea at his back.

'Sea Star!' he chuckled. 'I declare! You young ones pull just the right name out of the hat. How d'you do it?'

'It was Maureen,' Paul said, 'I was thinking of calling him Lonesome, but that was too sad of a name. Maureen just said his name right out. "Sea Star" she said, without even thinking.'

Paul shoved his toe in the sandy soil until he almost bent it back. 'Chief,' he said, 'will the Fire Department, you think, sell off the little colt? To us?'

The fire chief pinched his lip in thought. He closed his eyes for a minute. 'Sometimes,' he said, talking more to himself than to Paul and Maureen, 'sometimes the whole Department has to be called together so's a matter like this can be laid on the table for discussion.'

A little groan escaped Maureen.

'That's the way of it in most cases.' He was about to say more, but one of the roundup men came up, his eyes reddened.

'Got my specs knocked off during the ropin' this morning,' he said. 'Wonder, Chief, if you could do something about the nosepiece. It's broke.'

'Lucky you ain't bug-eyed,' the fire chief laughed, 'or you'd lost more'n your specs. I'll see they're fixed for you.'

He turned back to Paul and Maureen, going right on where he had left off. 'Then there are times,' he said, 'when a thing's so clear we'd only be wasting the men's time if we called up a meeting.'

'Yes?'

'This, now, is one of those times,' the chief said. 'A decision's got to be made quick when a pony's too young to fend for itself. By the way, where's Sea Star now?'

'He's in Misty's stall,' Maureen said.

'And,' Paul looked at the chief gravely, 'we've got ten dollars from the bronc-busting contest, because Mr Van

95

Meter wouldn't take the money to buy carrots for Misty.' Paul leaped to his feet as if an idea had just burst in his mind. 'Mr Van Meter said we might need it for something very special, and Sea Star's it!'

There was a waiting silence while the fire chief opened up a roll of peppermints and offered them to Maureen.

Paul clenched his fists in impatience. He made himself look straight into the fire chief's face. 'I reckon we'd need lots more than ten dollars,' he said bitterly. 'That is, if you'd sell him at all.'

Again the little whirlpool of silence while the chief absently folded the tinfoil around the peppermints. 'Now I view the matter like this,' he spoke at last. 'It's risky doin's, laying out money for a colt under three months. Mighty risky.' He pocketed the peppermints. 'No,' he said thoughtfully, 'the Fire Department wouldn't think of taking a cent over ten dollars for an orphan. I'm sure on it. Besides,' he added, 'that baby needs you two! Needs you bad.'

Paul and Maureen looked at each other. They wanted to thank the fire chief, but the words would not come, not even in a whisper.

Maureen found her voice first. 'Oh, Chief . . . !' she gulped, then could say no more. She threw her arms around his sun-creased neck and whispered an unintelligible thank-you in his ear.

Paul reached for one of the chief's hands and shook it hard. Then he slid his hand into the pocket of his jeans and took out the neatly folded ten-dollar bill.

13. NO ORNERY COLT FOR US

When Paul and Maureen returned home they found everything in the stall just as they had left it. The Arab mash untouched. The grass in the manger undisturbed. The water bucket full. And huddled in a corner of his stall, his head hanging low between his knees, Sea Star was sobbing out his lonesomeness in little colt whimpers.

Maureen's face went red and her lips tightened. 'We tried Grandpa's way,' she exploded. 'Now I'm going to fetch that bottle.'

'No, you ain't!' a voice behind them spoke sharply. Maureen hardly knew it for Grandpa's voice, and the sharpness hurt because it was so seldom used.

'I've been doctor-man to my hosses since afore you two was borned.' A fierce light of pride came into his eyes. 'In all my days I raised up only one colt to be mean and ornery, and I promised myself I'd nary do it again. Ye've got to trust me a mite longer. Ye've just got to. Chincoteague ponies is wiry. Tougher than you think.'

He stooped down on one knee and looked eye to eye with Sea Star, putting his gnarled fingers underneath the ringlets of the colt's mane.

The colt turned his head and sniffed. Memory told him there was no need to be afraid. He accepted Grandpa and Paul and Maureen as if they were no more nor less than the little wind that sifted in between the chinks in the siding.

Grandpa's eyes were unyielding as he straightened up. 'How many Pony Pennings,' he asked, 'can you two recomember?'

Paul and Maureen thought a moment, counting up on their fingers.

'Seven,' Paul said.

Maureen said, 'Seven for me, too.' Then at a surprised look from Grandpa, she changed her mind, 'Well, five for sure, Grandpa.'

'All right. Five times ye've *both* seed the wild ponies swimmed across from the island of Assateague to Chincoteague, ain't ye?'

The boy and girl nodded, while Sea Star tucked his forelegs beneath him and lay down on his side. He soon fell asleep to the drumming of Grandpa's voice.

'And five times,' the voice went on, 'ye've both seed the mares druv into the big pens and the colts cut out and druv into the little pens.'

Paul and Maureen nodded again, their eyes watching the foal's sides rise and fall.

'And each time after the cuttin' out was over with, ye've heard the colts bellerin' fer their mammas.'

Maureen clapped her hands to her ears as if she could hear the sound now.

Grandpa did not stop. 'The youngsters go millin' around in the pens hungerin' and thirstin' and refusin' to tech the water and grasses the firemen pervides. But,' and here Grandpa began rubbing the bristles of his ear, 'but before the week is out, what *always* happens?'

'The colts are eating nice as you please,' smiled Paul.

'That's the right answer, Paul! Now I know you're a hoss-man!'

Maureen slipped her hand inside Grandpa's. 'We'll wait, Grandpa, afore we think about that nursing bottle again. Sea Star'll be eating like a stallion by the time the week is over, won't he?'

Friday passed. The crowds trickled out of the Pony Penning Grounds and over the causeway to the mainland.

Saturday came, and the mares and stallions were let out of the big pens and driven back home to the island of the wild things. The few unsold colts were driven back, too. They were older, wiser, able to fend for themselves.

At Pony Ranch, Sea Star dozed the hours away. Unlike the other colts, he seemed to have grown littler, younger.

Saturday night came. Darkness drifted down softly over Chincoteague. The moon rose slowly, unrolling a broad carpet of silver out across the Atlantic.

It found Paul's bed and tickled his face with its beams. He turned to the wall, but the moon would not be put aside. It rode through his sleep. In his dreams he was flying on a moonbeam, lighting a path through the woods for the Phantom, lighting a schoolyard in New York where crowds of children were pressing in on Misty, stroking her neck with grubby fingers. He was lighting a desk in Richmond where Uncle Clarence Lee sat bent over papers and books.

Then suddenly the moonbeam became a silver lance and Sea Star was dancing in the prick of light it made. Now the silver lance was cutting the grass in wide swaths, showing

the colt how tender it was, and soon Sea Star understood.
He began ripping it, grinding it with his baby teeth.

Paul awoke. He listened sharply. It was only the wind
shaking the pine needles.

He jumped from his bed. He looked out over the flat
tongue of land where the silver plane had landed. The
moon was still shining brightly. He dressed and quietly
opened the door of his room. The guinea hens were begin-
ning to wake. They were clacking loudly. Paul was glad.
Now his footsteps would not waken Grandma and Grandpa.
He passed their closed door. He came to Maureen's door and
almost collided with her. There she was, tiptoeing out into
the hall.

'What you fixing to do?' whispered Maureen.

Paul's sheepish grin was lost in the dark. 'Sh!' he said, putting his finger to his lips. 'I'm going to make a warm gruel.'

Maureen's mouth flew open. 'Why, that's exactly what I was fixing to do!'

In single file they stepped wide of the boards that creaked and came down into the kitchen. A light glowed brightly over the stove and there was Grandma stirring oatmeal porridge and reading her Sunday school lesson as she stirred.

'Well, I never!' she gasped at the two surprised faces before her. 'I thought I was seeing owls. I just got up early to prepare my lesson,' she exclaimed. 'Come sit down and eat a morsel of porridge. Though I *was* fixing it for someone else – a four-footed critter.'

Maureen caught Grandma's hand and clasped it tight between both of hers. 'Oh, Grandma,' she said, 'you're the understandingest grandma in the whole wide world.'

Paul fumbled under the sink where the pots and pans were kept. He found an old one that had lost a handle and held it up for Grandma.

She looked at it and nodded. Then she spooned out a big helping of the steaming meal and sprinkled a handful of brown sugar over the top of it.

'Go along, you two. Our breakfast can wait until after you coax Sea Star. Always and always it'll be the same here, I reckon. The ponies comes first, then the people. Go along while I memorize my text.' Her words trailed out after them, '"And the angel of the Lord stood among the myrtle trees . . ."'

14. THE GENTLEMAN FROM KENTUCKY

Sea Star refused the porridge.

Maureen said, 'He spits it out as if 'twas vinegar.'

'He was somethin'!' Paul said. 'Just look at him now. Ribs showing like a squeeze box.' He turned away, stumbling across the barnyard, and headed for the piney woods.

Maureen followed at a distance. The sun was rising. Long shafts of sunlight slid through the trees, gilding one side, leaving the other black. The piney litter underfoot deadened the sound of their feet. Maureen watched Paul's fists go to his eyes and brush something away with the back of his hand.

'Ain't the cobwebs bothersome this time of morning?' she said, coming up to him.

'Sure are,' Paul replied, keeping his face ahead. 'For a girl, you're right observing.'

'Oh, thank you, Paul. I didn't aim to be a tag-along, but I couldn't bear not to come. I figured you'd be brooding something in your mind.'

Paul slowed his steps. 'I been brooding all right.'

'Sure enough?'

The boy nodded.

'What you decided, Paul?'

Paul's voice began to sound more like his own. There was a wild note of hope in it. 'One Pony Penning a gentleman was here all the way from Lexington, Kentucky. And he got to talking manlike to me and Grandpa. He had a big nurse-mare farm.'

'A nurse-mare farm?'

'A nurse-mare farm.'

'What's that?'

'Quit interrupting, Maureen; I'm trying to figure something out. You just listen.'

'All right, I will. But oh, Paul, make it good!'

Paul cuffed the pine branches with his hands as he walked, sending dewdrops flying in every direction. It seemed to ease his feelings and loosen his tongue. 'This gentleman,' he said, 'owned lots of draft mares and jennies, and they most always had young 'uns tagging at their heels. Then when a fine Thoroughbred colt from one of the big racing stables near by lost its mamma, why, then the gentleman would rent out one of his mares and the little Thoroughbred would eat off her. He'd grow big and strong.'

'Oh, Paul! It's beautiful!' Maureen heaved a loud sigh. 'Now all we got to do is rope a mare over on Assateague and rent her from the Fire Department.'

Paul snorted in disgust. ''Taint as easy as that. A wild mare'd kick the living daylights out of an orphan colt. She'd want her own colt back, or none at all. She might even kill another colt.'

'What if . . .' Maureen gasped with the wonder of the idea that had come to her. 'What if the mare couldn't kick? What if her heel string was cut and she couldn't light out with the other heel?'

Paul let out a low whistle. 'Why, she wouldn't have a leg to stand on!'

Maureen was beside herself with excitement. 'Let's go right back and . . .'

'Wait!' said Paul. 'The man told me and Grandpa lots of other things. He said that if the nurse mare didn't want to adopt a strange colt, she could hold herself all tense-like and the milk just wouldn't come out. And besides, the mare with the cut heel has still got a mighty good set of teeth and she could bite. Bite hard.' Paul opened his jaws and snapped them sharply together. The sound sent a shiver through Maureen.

'What we got to do,' Paul said, 'is to make that mare *want* to take on Sea Star for her very own. *That's* what we go to do.'

For several minutes they followed along the winding path in silence.

Maureen slipped past Paul, her bare feet making no noise at all. 'Hmpf!' she taunted. 'If your man from Kentucky was so awful smart, how did he do it?'

Paul did not answer right away. He kicked a pine cone along the path with his toes until it scuttered behind a tree trunk. He peered into a deserted redbird's nest. 'I recomember now!' he said as if he had found the answer among the twigs and rootlets of the nest. 'He told us he used to rub the colt all over with sheep dip. Then he'd rub the mare's nose with it, too. He'd trick her into thinking the colt was hers 'cause they smelled the same.'

Now the words were tumbling over each other. 'He told about a lady stable owner, too, who was in the perfume business, and she rubbed a mare and an orphan colt with the same perfume, and the mare took on the colt.'

Maureen halted, nodding to herself as if she had discovered something very wise and secret.

'Paul! Whiff! Like this.' She drew the pungent odour of the myrtle trees deep into her lungs, and laughed as she blew it out again. 'What smells so good and perfumey as our own myrtle leaves?'

The wind had picked up the fragrance from the thicket of myrtle trees ahead and was blowing it in their faces. Now they both threw back their heads like colts and snuffed it in greedily.

A muffled, rustling sound! A crackling of brush! A sudden stirring in the clump of myrtles!

Startled, Maureen touched Paul's arm and pointed to the swaying branches. They both hung back, motionless, listening. The feathered *whish* of bird wings? The pawing of a wild deer? An otter? Questions went unasked as the sound faded out, then began again.

'Might be Grandma's lesson come true,' whispered Maureen in awe, 'might be the angel of the Lord standing among the myrtle trees.'

'It *is*!' shouted Paul. 'It's Grandpa Beebe!'

15. A HAUNTIN' SMELL O'
MYRTLE LEAVES

There came an answering shout, and a familiar face with white, spiky whiskers peered out of the frame of myrtle leaves. The face rimpled into a sudden smile, and a voice rolled out strong:

'Oh, they're wild and woolly and full of fleas
And never been curried below the knees . . .'

'Childern!' laughed Grandpa. 'Ye come just in time to help. I got some empty gunny sacks here and I want 'em filled plum full o' . . .'

'Myrtle leaves!' cried Paul and Maureen in the same breath.

Grandpa nodded in surprise as he gave one sack to Paul and another to Maureen. Then he reached toward a branch, talking as he stripped the leaves. 'Once there was a gentleman here from . . .'

'Lexington, Kentucky!' Paul filled in the words, grinning.

Grandpa's head turned around and his eyes went wide. 'And this gentleman had a . . .''

'Nurse-mare farm!' Paul and Maureen shouted in unison, like actors in a play.

Both hands suddenly went up to Grandpa's ears and he began rubbing the bristles hard. 'I ain't a-pridin' on myself,' he chuckled, 'but now I know fer sure there's somethin' of the best of me in the both of ye!' His laughter bubbled low, then rang out in the stillness of the woods.

It was good to have work to do. Old gnarled fingers and young smooth ones worked swiftly, stripping off the long narrow leaves, filling the bags.

Grandpa brought out his knife and cut off vines that got in their way. 'I couldn't sleep last night for worritin' about that little fella,' he said. 'Whenever I dropt off, I drempt. I'd be combin' his curly mane with my fingers and feelin' of the little ribs stickin' out like the ribs of Grandma's bumberella. Then right smack out o' nowhere came the man from Kentucky nosin' into my dreams. He tolded all over again how that lady rubbed perfume on a nurse mare and an orphan colt. And next think I knew, I was sittin' up in bed a-whisperin' to myself, "What in tunket has a more hauntin' smell as our own . . ."'

'Myrtle leaves!' exploded Paul and Maureen.

Grandpa's eyes twinkled. 'Yes, sir! There's somethin' in this mental telegraphy all right.'

Hands worked faster and faster, filling the bags. Now they were half full.

'Jumpin' mullets! I clean forgot to tell ye who the nurse mare's goin' to be.' Grandpa's voice rose and quickened with his fingers. 'Last night while the moon was ridin' high, I snuck out the house in my bare feet, horse-backs over to Wilbur Wimbrow's and fetches him out o' bed.

'"Wilbur, I says to him, "little Sea Star is bad off. He's gettin' mighty poor. Won't eat. How about puttin' him to the mare that got her heel cut?"'

'What'd he say?' Maureen glanced up, watching Grandpa's face intently.

'Wilbur was never one to mince words. He says to me, "Clarence, you an' me is 'bout the oldest roundup men we got in Chincoteague, and we both knows mares is notionate critters. They take a notion they don't like a colt and they'll have no truck with it." Then he minded me of the time we tried to get a mare to be a foster mamma and she jest skinned back her ears and lit out with her heels and like to a-kilt the little stranger.'

Maureen gasped.

107

'But we took a lantern out to the barn and I made sure that
the mare was still favourin' her near hind leg. Then I looked
at her milk bag and saw 'twas swelled with milk. Wilbur,
he followed my glance.'

'What'd he say?' Paul asked, scarcely above a whisper.

'He just sort of grunted. Had to admit she wasn't lackin'
for milk. "But will she give it?" he asked.

'Then I told him how we'd smash up some myrtle leaves
and souse the colt all over with the oily smell of 'em, and
we'd rub the mare's nose with it too, and maybe she'd
think 'twas her own colt come back to her.'

Paul and Maureen let out a deep sigh.

'Stop, childern!' commanded Grandpa. 'We got enough

leaves here to souse a whole flock of ponies. Let's git a-goin'.'

As they hurried back along the path, Grandpa forgot all about breakfast. He was busy with plans. 'Maureen, you bare-back over to Wilbur Wimbrow's. He's waitin' to help ye with the mare. Me and Paul will fix up the colt till he smells like a whole clump of myrtle. Then we'll hist him into the truck and bring him to his new mamma.'

When Maureen was up on Watch Eyes and had gathered the reins in one hand and taken the bag of myrtle under her arm, Grandpa waited a moment before opening the gate for her. He beckoned Paul over to his side. 'If you two was jes' little children,' he spoke to them slowly, thoughtfully, 'I wouldn't have you to worry. But bein' as ye're nigh growed up, I got to tell you this idee *might* not work.' Then his voice rolled out like a steam calliope. 'Git a-goin', child. What's keepin' ye? Are ye glued to the earth?' And he slapped Watch Eyes on the rump.

Maureen spurred him with her heels. 'Giddap, Watch Eyes. Faster! Faster! You can help.'

Watch Eyes liked the idea. He stretched out as if he were racing his own shadow. It was all Maureen could do to turn him in at Wimbrow's lane. He wanted to go on and on into the morning.

The clatter of hooves brought Mr Wimbrow out of his house, carrying a steaming pail in one hand and a wooden bowl with a potato masher in the other.

'Morning, Maureen,' he said. 'Put Watch Eyes in that stall next to the mare.'

Maureen looked up into the lean, weathered face of the roundup man. She gave him a small nervous smile as she led Watch Eyes to the empty stall.

'I'll need you to grind up the leaves,' Mr Wimbrow said. 'Here's our potato masher and a bowl. I was just fixing to bathe the mare's heel. You can sit in the doorway and work. It'll do the mare good to begin getting a whiff of the myrtle.'

Maureen pounded and beat the leaves. The fragrance filled her nostrils until it wiped out the smell of the disinfectant Mr Wimbrow was using.

Her eyes slid over the mare as she worked. She saw how Mr Wimbrow had tied her to a corner of the stall to keep her from moving about and using the hurt leg. She saw the mare turn her head to watch what was going on. But there was no sharp interest in the way she watched. It was the same look that Sea Star had – a sad, dulled look as if nothing at all mattered.

'This cut ain't healing like it should,' Mr Wimbrow worried aloud, sloshing the water over it with his hand. 'Some say we should put ice packs onto it. Some say we'd ought to plunge it in hot salt water. I'm doing the best I know how.' He sighed, feeling along the tendon. 'But what I think is, she's a-grievin' so she ain't even trying to get well.'

He threw the bucket of water out of the door and came back to tie up the heel with a clean bandanna. 'Likely it'd be better if you rubbed her nose with the myrtle,' he said. 'She's still got the wildness in her. She thinks of me as someone who keeps bothering that hurt foot. But you, now,' he smiled down at Maureen, 'you can be a messenger from the woods, bringing gifts of myrtle.'

Maureen's hand trembled a little as she scooped up a mound of crushed leaves and slowly went around to the mare's head. She held out her hand just far enough away so the mare had to reach for it. Suddenly the nostrils began to quiver. That familiar fragrance! It seemed to stir memories of the warm places, deep in the woods; memories of the life-giving myrtle, green when all the grasses were dried. She lipped a taste of it, and as she rolled it on her tongue Maureen rubbed oily fingers around one of the mare's nostrils. At the touch of fingers she drew back snorting, her muscles twitching in fright.

Maureen's heart was thumping wildly now. She waited for the mare's fear to pass, waited seconds before the

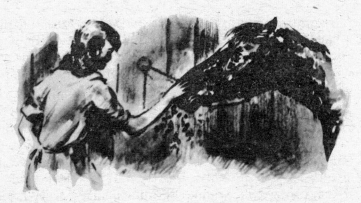

quivering nose reached out again and she could rub the other nostril.

Back at Pony Ranch every hand was busy. Paul grinding the leaves in Grandma's clam grinder, Grandma sewing bags of cheesecloth, and Grandpa stuffing them with myrtle.

'If anybody'd ever said I'd be sewing on the Sabbath day,' Grandma said to herself as her needle flew, 'I'd have low'd my head in shame. But here I am, sewing for all I'm worth, and out in a stable against my ruthers. Queer how a young 'un can nudge in and upset all your notions.'

'That's the way of it,' Grandpa chuckled softly. He nodded his head in Paul's direction. 'And don't it beat all how fast Paul's a-grindin'? The sweat's rollin' off him. If 'twas clams, now, instead of myrtle leaves, he'd be cool as a cowcumber and there'd be mighty few clams grinded.'

'That's what I admire about Paul,' Grandma said with certainty. 'When something important's at stake, he pitches in.'

A look of understanding shuttled between Paul and Grandma.

All this while Sea Star drowsed in a corner of the stall. The smell of myrtle excited no memories in him. Sometimes he cried in his sleep and woke himself up. Then listlessly he would watch the strange doings of the humans.

'Now, Paul,' Grandpa said, 'ye can grab a bag of myrtle and rub Star from stem to stern whilst I hold him. Mind ye, don't miss a hair.' Putting one hand under the foal's muzzle and grasping his tail with the other, Grandpa lifted him to his feet. 'Go to it, Paul. I got him steadied.'

Paul began rubbing, timidly at first, then vigorously.

'Why, I believe he likes it,' Paul laughed, a little awed, and he began asking questions like sparks bursting from a fire. 'Does he look more fawn than colt to you? His star, it shines bright on his forehead, see? What makes colts' knees so funny and knobby? Reckon he'll have a left mane like Misty's?'

There was no time for Grandma or Grandpa to answer one question before the next fell.

The boy stopped a moment, standing quietly. Then he squatted on his heels and went to work on the foal's face.

'Look at me, Sea Star,' he said. 'When Misty comes back home, you and she can be a team. Misty and Star. Sound pretty to you? And you can run like birds together and you can raise up foals of your own, and Maureen and I can race you both and we won't care which wins. And . . . I guess I need a fresh bag, Grandma. This one's all squinched out.'

Occasionally Sea Star fought for his freedom, but it was a weak little fight, as if he knew he had no place to go if he were free.

He let Paul rub his colty whiskers with myrtle. He let him put some of it in his mouth, but he neither chewed nor swallowed it.

'Guess you won't be needing me any more,' Grandma said, picking up the clam grinder and her spool of thread. 'I'll go in and read over my lesson just once more. Be sure to come back in time to get me to my class,' she called over her shoulder.

Grandpa nodded absent-mindedly. Then he buried his nose in Sea Star's coat. 'Yep,' he sniffed, 'if I closed my eyes, I'd think I was right spang in a clump of myrtle. Now, Paul, carry him to the truck. I'll hyper on ahead and let down the ramp.'

All during the ride to Wimbrow's, Paul quieted Sea Star with his voice. 'You just lean up against me,' he said. 'Never knew the roads were so bumpity. But I'll stay close to you for comfort. Once I spent a whole night in a truck with Misty. I'd do it for you, too,' he breathed into the silky ear.

16. LET'S DO SOMETHING

Inside Wilbur Wimbrow's gate Paul set the colt down on the grass. To Paul's surprise, he followed along to the barn as if an invisible lead rope held them together.

Looking at the weak little colt, Mr Wimbrow shook his head. 'Sure is slab-sided,' he said. 'Let's *do* something!' He turned to Grandpa. 'Ought we to blindfold the mare?'

''Tain't no use. Sea Star's about the colour o' her own colt. We'll coax in with him and put him right onto her. Maureen and Paul, you kin look on – if you back up against the wall and stay put.'

Matters were out of Paul's and Maureen's hands now. All they could do was to watch the two men wise in the ways of animals.

The stall came alive with expectancy. Mr Wimbrow tuned his voice down low. He was trying to make it sound natural, but Paul and Maureen felt a tightness in it. 'I'll hold the mare's head so she can't turn round and bite,' he said. 'Clarence, you put the little fellow where he belongs.'

He followed his own directions. He took hold of the halter rope close to the mare's chin. He stood there, waiting, without speaking any more.

Grandpa drew in his breath sharply, overcome by the importance of the next few moments. He placed his roughened hand on Sea Star's neck, urging the little fellow forward, inside the doorway of the stall. He turned him gently around, so that Sea Star's nose was at the mare's flanks.

Then he took his hand away.

There was no sound, except for a greenhead fly drumming against a water pail. No one moved. Not the two men nor the boy or girl. The world outside did not exist. There was just a dull, spiritless mare, a weak and hungry foal that did not belong to her, and over all, the pungent fragrance of myrtle oil.

Now the mare filled in the silence. With a sound no bigger than a whisper she began snuffing and blowing and snuffing in again. She tried to turn her head.

Wilbur Wimbrow looked at Grandpa, his eyebrows asking a question.

Grandpa Beebe's head nodded yes.

Mr Wimbrow let go the rope. The mare could turn her head now. She brought it around slowly toward Sea Star, looking. Now her breathing was quick, as if she had just come in winded from a gallop. And then in the middle of a breath came a quiver of sound. It was like a plucked violin string. It was pain and joy and hunger and thirst all mixed into one trembling note. She and the colt were one! A high neigh of ecstasy escaped her. Fiercely she began licking Sea Star's coat, scolding him tenderly with her tongue all the while.

'*My sakes! Look at your coat, will you! Scraggy as anything. No shine to it at all. You been neglected. But I'll make you shining again!*' Her tongue strokes said all that and more. She almost upset Sea Star with her mothering. She was shoving him around to suit herself. He was swaying like a blade of grass in the wind.

Paul and Maureen could hardly breathe. Every sound, every motion, seemed sharp and clear. The fly buzzing against the pail, and from some distance away a mockingbird weaving a morning song.

Now Sea Star was questing with his nose, with his lips, moving slowly in toward the mare, drawn in toward her, crying a thin, plaintive mew. Suddenly the crying became a joyous snort – a snort of discovery. He had found the warm bag of milk! He was suckling!

Excitement ran through the stall like flame. Suck! Suck!

Grunt and suck! A little brush of a tail flicking back and forth to the rhythm. It said, more plainly than any words, 'This is good, good, *good*, I tell you.'

For a long time no one spoke. It was enough happiness just to listen to the smothered grunting and to watch the flappety tail. At last Grandpa heaved a great sigh and smiled from one to the other as if they had all come through a great crisis together.

'Jest listen to that little fellow goozle,' he said. 'That mare gives a lot o' milk, too. Never knew one to take on a colt like that.'

'He'll never be no stunted colt now,' Mr Wimbrow said.

'Less'n he drinks so much he'll get stunted carrying it!' laughed Grandpa, relief written on his face.

The mare paid no heed to the voices at all. She had so much to do. Licking and brushing Sea Star's coat to make up for the lost days, and talking all the while in little nickers.

Paul swallowed two or three times before he could make his voice sound like his own. 'Sea Star's having his Pony Penning dinner today,' he said shakily.

Maureen nodded happily, 'And didn't that mare have sharp smellers? She put me in mind of Grandma.'

Grandpa caught his breath at mention of Grandma. He squared his hat on his head. 'We got to get on, Wilbur. Ida's a great one for gettin' to her Sunday school class on time.' He took a final look at the mare. 'Most always ye got to watch a nurse mare and an orphan for two-three days afore ye can leave 'em together, but the way she's chattin' over little personal matters with him . . . well, he ain't no lost star now.'

Mr Wimbrow nodded. 'Soon as I think the mare can hobble along on her own power, I'll lead 'em both over to Pony Ranch. The children can keep her until Sea Star grows up.'

Paul walked out of the stall alongside Mr Wimbrow.

'We'll be glad to pay rent for her like the big racing stables do,' he said. ' 'Course, we can't pay so much.'

Mr Wimbrow roughed his hand over Paul's head. 'Really should be the other way around,' he said. 'The colt saved the mare's life. He come just in the nick of time. She's got something to get well for now.'

17. OPEN THE GATE

Grandma was under the pine trees, stirring something in an iron kettle over a fire. She seemed neither ready to go to church nor ready to stay at home. She was wearing her Sunday hat, and over her Sunday dress she had tied a big apron. The smell of chicken steaming with wild onions curled out of the pot. As Grandpa's truck drove in she stopped stirring and waited for the family to come to her.

'You don't need to tell me,' she cried. 'It's *good* news! Paul's hair is rumpled as a kingfisher's topknot, Grandpa's wearing his hat backside to, and Maureen's been twisting her curls the wrong way. You don't need to let out a peep,' She said with shining eyes. 'Sea Star's eating! Now we're going to eat, too. We're going to have us a real old-timey Pony Penning feast. You know, you forgot all about breakfast.'

Paul and Maureen laughed. They *had* forgotten about breakfast.

Grandpa rubbed his stomach and smacked his lips in pleased anticipation. 'To me it smells like outdoor pot pie, simmerin' full of goodness.'

'Might be,' Grandma said.

Maureen looked into the pot and began stirring. 'But, Grandma, what about your Sunday school class?'

'The Lord understood, and so did Mrs Tilley. She's going to substitute teach for me.'

'Ida!' Grandpa scolded in mock sternness, 'I never thought I'd live to see the day when you'd get high-toney on yer own family.'

'High-toney?'

119

'Yep, high-toney. Seems to me that when ye wears yer best hat to a outdoor picnic . . .''

Grandma threw her apron over her face and laughed until the tears came. And soon the whole pine grove echoed with laughter.

'Here, Maureen, lay my hat in on my bed. Then you can

take the biscuits out of the oven and dish up the Seven Top turnip greens. Clarence, you and Paul slick up. Oh, I haven't been so happy in a week! I've got a hungry family again.'

When the picnic table was set and the plates heaped with the chicken pot pie and greens and hot biscuits, they all sat down, Grandpa and Grandma on one bench, Paul and Maureen on the other. Hungry as they were, they did not eat at once. They turned to Grandma, waiting for a word from her.

Grandpa's voice boomed his loudest to hide his real feelings. 'Ida, I reckon ye can say grace at a picnic jest as well as to any other time.'

Grandma stood up at the end of the table. Her eyes began to twinkle. 'I feel like a colt,' she admitted almost shyly. 'You know how choicy they are when first they begin to eat? You give 'em some grasses, and they go picking out certain ones that seem saltier than the others, and maybe they hunt for a little bunch of lespedeza.'

Paul laughed. 'That's just the way they do, Grandma.'

'Well, so long as you're not my regular Sunday school class, I'm going to pull out wisps of goodness from the Good Book here and there. 'Tain't the formal way to do, I know. But it's mighty satisfying.'

Grandma was shy no longer. She looked up beyond the tallest pine tree, right into the deep sky. She waited for the words to form in her mind. Then she sang them out:

'"The angel of the Lord stood among the myrtle trees."'

Maureen's and Paul's eyes met and smiled knowingly.

'"And the morning stars sang together, and all the sons of God shouted for joy."'

Grandpa's hand went up to the bristles in his ears. 'Ida,' he chortled, 'that's a hull sermon of itself! I like 'em short like that. If I could be in your class, don't know but what I'd be first there ever' Sunday. I'd even brave all them womenfolks.'

Grandma's face beamed as she ladled chicken gravy over every plate. Then she sat down.

No one had to be urged to eat. Plates, wiped clean with biscuits, came up for second and third helpings.

'A good thing biscuits don't have pits inside 'em,' Paul grinned, reaching for another. 'Nobody can count how many I've had.'

They ate until they could eat no more. And then instead of going off to chores, they stayed a moment as if caught in some spell no one wanted to break.

'This week is embroidered in my heart,' Grandma said.

'Just think of little Misty sending Clarence Lee to college!'

Grandpa chuckled. 'Y'know,' he said, 'I kin see the diploma hangin' onto the parlour wall already, and writ on it as plain as plain is the name, "Clarence Lee Beebe, Jr." And I'm goin' to print out Misty's name alongside it. And that's all I'll ever read on it,' he laughed. 'College people wastes words.'

Paul swung one leg over the picnic bench and faced out to sea. A silence washed over them, a cosy silence, not sad at all. And running through it were the tiniest sounds that made it even cosier. The wind riffling the pine needles and rustling along the grasses. A duckling trying its wings. Guinea hens scratching. And deep in the woods a wren spilling a waterfall of notes.

Grandpa dropped his voice to fit the quiet. 'Me and yer Grandma have had a good many head of children,' he mused to himself, 'but when each one went off to work or to war, we always got a little dread inside us. But then . . ."

'Then what?' asked Maureen.

'Always somebody was left behind to stay a spell with us. Even when all our children was growed up and didn't need us, then you two come along and the empty feelin' was gone.'

Paul let out a cry, cut off in the middle. He leaped to his feet. 'Look!' he yelled. 'Look what's coming!'

Maureen whirled around, almost falling off the bench in her haste. Coming into view at the bend of the lane was a tall, lank man leading a splashy brown-and-white mare. The mare limped a little on her near hind foot, and her head kept turning around as she hobbled along. But it was not her foot that worried her. It was a little brown colt nuzzling along beside her.

'Ahoy, Paul! Ahoy, Maureen!' yelled Wilbur Wimbrow. 'Come get your colt and mare. I got to go down the bay oysterin' tomorrow. I can't be wastin' my time on these two. They're yours!'

123

Paul and Maureen flew to meet them.

'You – know – what?' Paul asked, a little breathless as he ran.

'What?' puffed Maureen.

'Sea Star's come to adopt *us*!'

He called to Mr Wimbrow. 'We're coming! We're coming to open the gate!'

Four miles off the eastern shore of Virginia lies the tiny, wind-rippled isle of Chincoteague. It is only seven miles long and averages but twenty-one inches above the sea.

Assateague Island, however, is thirty-three miles long. Just as Paul Beebe says, Assateague is an outrider, protecting little Chincoteague from the rough seas of the Atlantic. The outer island is a wildlife refuge for wild geese and ducks and the wild ponies.

Misty of Chincoteague

MARGUERITE HENRY

Just off the coast of Virginia lie the islands of Chincoteague and Assateague. On Assateague, ponies run wild all the year – except on Pony Penning Day, when the men of Chincoteague come over to round up the herd. The wild and beautiful Phantom had always escaped them, but young Paul Beebe and his sister, Maureen are determined to tame her. Paul miraculously succeeds in bringing Phantom and her colt Misty back to Chincoteague.

This is the story of the two children and of the joy their ponies bring them. But even more, it is the story of Misty, who was theirs completely, and of Phantom, whose heart they never quite captured.

King of the Wind

MARGUERITE HENRY

Sham was faster than the wind, for he bore the white spot on his heel, symbol of speed. But upon his chest was the wheat-ear, mark of ill-luck – these two signs were to rule his life.

He was born in the Royal Stables of Morocco and was prized for his beauty and speed. Then circumstance leads him to France and England where disaster follows cruel disaster. But his spirit cannot be broken. . .

And with him always is Agba, the Arab horse-boy who loves him.

Born Free

The Story of Elsa

JOY ADAMSON

Elsa was born free, a lioness of Kenya, but when she was several weeks old, her mother was killed. So the Adamsons adopted her. Elsa slept on their beds, licked their faces with her sandpaper tongue, and knocked them to the ground with her paw as her own special joke! She chased elephants, stalked rhinos and played hide and seek with gazelles.

But the time came when she grew restless, and the Adamsons decided to return her to her natural life in the wild. Their attempts were hazardous and painful, for Elsa had to be accepted by her own kind, and more vital, she had to learn to kill for herself if she were to survive.

Joy Adamson's famous books about Elsa, *Born Free* and *Living Free* have inspired two of the most popular animal films of all time. *Living Free* is also an Armada Lion.